Exposed

Atlantic City's Most Wanted #7

Charity Parkerson

Punk & Sissy Publications

COPYRIGHT

—Warning: This book is intended for readers over the age of 18. Some of my books contain allusions to past abuse and trauma.

CONTENTS

Introduction

HE DIDN'T THINK THERE could be anything worse than going to the wedding of the one who got away. Then he saw HIM.

Kace recently reconnected with the one man he's ever loved. He's too late to be more than friends, but he'll take it. Of course, going to the guy's wedding kind of sucks. But the last thing he sees coming is someone trying to set him up with a very familiar face—the man he hires on a regular basis to cuddle with him.

It's obvious Kace can't be more mortified by seeing Jamison outside of their appointments. Jamison tries his best to put Kace at ease. Things don't go well. From there, every encounter is a rollercoaster of surprises. While Jamison can't wait to see what happens next, he never saw his past coming back to haunt him. Now Kace might be the only good thing that ever happens to him again.

Exposed is the seventh book in Charity Parkerson's Atlantic City's Most Wanted series. These are sexy and sometimes dark stories where the richest and most dangerous men in Atlantic City meet their match. These are best enjoyed when read in order.

CHAPTER ONE

"DID YOU KNOW MY nephew gets paid to cuddle people for a living?"

Everyone has a God-given talent, whether or not they realize it. Jamison just happened to be born cuddly, compassionate, and completely shameless. It was the perfect combination in his profession. Still, he had to admit it was a tad uncomfortable to have his aunt do her best to set him up at a wedding with one of his clients. Not that she knew that part. Jamison did his best to be polite and kind while not losing a customer or insulting his favorite aunt. She was his only aunt, but still his favorite. Unfortunately, Dr. Kace Brightly looked downright horrified, and Jamison had no clue how to salvage the situation.

Sadly, his aunt Haven thrived on scandalizing people and today, the poor doctor looked to be her next victim. "Isn't that something? Who knew?"

Jamison jumped in. "There are several scientific studies that show cuddling lowers stress, which in turn helps lower blood pressure, cholesterol, and helps with depression. A multitude of things, actually."

"That's what they say."

Yeah. He would never hear from Kace again. Kace sounded like he wanted to die.

Jamison set his champagne aside. "Would you like to dance?"

Kace's eerily light green eyes slid toward the dance floor, as if calculating which was worse—this conversation or a private one.

"Sure." He did not sound enthused.

Still, Jamison tried to keep up the smiles. He had to smooth things over. While he had other clients, and he made a great living, he couldn't start losing them over unexpected encounters. Jamison flashed his aunt a smile. She beamed back at him, certain she had found a love match. He met Kace's stare and motioned toward the dance floor.

Kace moved that way, looking like he walked on wooden legs. This wasn't going well. Then he had Kace's in his arms and Jamison recalled exactly why he was so determined not to lose Kace. The guy fit. It was like he was meant to be right where he was.

"So, James. How have you been?"

The way Kace emphasized the name Jamison used with clients spoke volumes. This was likely beyond repair. "I hope you understand why I have to keep my real name a secret. You're a good person and seem sane, but that's not true of everyone. There are people who think once they've paid me, they own me. It's not safe."

"Great. It sounds like I've been hiring a prostitute."

Damn. This had never happened to him. "Did you just call me a whore?"

Kace looked horrified. "No. I meant the way you said that. That's the exact reason prostitutes and strippers use fake names. I just never realized how creepy it is for me to hire you. Now, pathetic. I knew that much."

Jamison hated everything about this. "It's not creepy or pathetic. You have an important, stressful, and extremely busy job. I doubt you've had time to look elsewhere, and I meant what I said to Haven." The more he thought about it, the more Kace's reaction pissed him off. "You know what? Don't hire me again. If you want to think what I do is dumb or embarrassing or whatever, I'm not about to beg you to see me as a real person working like everyone else. Just because you're a doctor, that doesn't give you any right to look down on people. So, go fuck yourself." Jamison walked away, leaving Kace on the dance floor alone. He made a beeline for his aunt. He didn't let her worried expression slow him.

Jamison bent and hugged her. "It was good to see you. I have an appointment."

"You have always given the best hugs."

The pressure in Jamison's chest eased. Haven was a good person. "I love you. Be careful going home."

"I love you too and you too."

Jamison quickly headed for the door. He wasn't one to lose his temper, but damn. Jamison had been nothing but nice to Kace. He didn't deserve to be made to feel less than just because Kace was embarrassed. Kace could find someone else. Jamison was hardly the only one in the field. Once someone knew where to look, it wasn't hard to find just about any service.

Jamison climbed into his truck and pulled out his phone. It took him a second to log in to his web account so he could get to his client list. He blocked Kace and then moved to wipe his information. Jamison's finger hovered over the delete option. His shoulders fell. He unblocked the contact. While he was insulted and upset, Jamison wasn't an asshole. He doubted Kace would ever reach out again anyhow. Jamison's eyes fell closed. He was always the weak one.

As much as Kace wanted to rush after Jamison, Haven already looked way too curious. There was no avoiding her. She would likely run after him if he tried to make a break for it. That would be one hell of a scene at her son's wedding. Instead, he motioned for her to join him on the floor.

A huge grin lit her face as she took Jamison's place. It hurt his chest how much she looked like her son, Joesph. That was the gist of things. This was Joesph's wedding. The one who got away. Kace had already felt like he was dying before Haven dragged him to meet her nephew, then his humiliation had been complete. Nothing had shone a light on how pathetic and empty his life was the way this entire wedding had. He wanted to go home. There was nothing for him here. Unfortunately, nothing waited at home for him either. At this point, it was whatever, so he danced.

"Okay. Spill."

He wouldn't play dumb. Haven was too relentless. "I think I insulted his job."

"Why would you do that? Just a few minutes ago, you agreed science backed his profession."

Kace felt worse by the second. It hurt his chest, thinking about losing the service Jamison provided. He didn't want to go through those beginning stages again, where he felt humiliated by his needs with someone new. Jamison had always made him feel like it wasn't a job for him—like he wanted to snuggle with Kace too. "I'll reach out and apologize."

Her gaze sharpened. "I didn't see him give you his number."

Damn. He had to be fast on his feet with Haven. Kace pulled his most pathetic face. "I hoped you'd give it to me."

She studied him for a second before brightening. "Sure. I know you're a good one. You won't use it to stalk him or anything. Isn't he gorgeous, though? He's my brother-in-law's son. The Drake gene pool is strong as hell. Every one of them ended up with those light blue eyes. Of course, Jamison took after his mom's dad with that cuddly build."

"I always thought Joesph looks a lot like you."

Haven beamed. "That's sweet since I raised a gorgeous son. You never met his father, though. He'd already passed before you dated Joesph."

"That was a long time ago. You're a beautiful woman. I'm sure you have tons of men beating down your door."

Haven's smile turned sad. "Some people can't be replaced. I'll never let some mediocre man destroy my image of a good marriage. I got lucky the first time around. The odds of lightning striking twice are pretty damn slim."

Somehow, Kace kept nodding and listening while his entire brain screamed. What were the odds lightning would strike twice? He was at the wedding of the man who Kace had been certain was the one for him. Now what? He was doomed to die alone.

Songs changed.

"Oh, do you mind if I steal a dance with my new son-in-law?"

Kace pasted on the same smile he used when dealing with patients. "Sure." This actually gave him the perfect opportunity to sneak out without being noticed.

"Great. We'll talk again later."

Kace kept smiling and nodding. Relief poured through him as he walked away. He didn't make it far before a strong arm encircled his waist.

"Dr. Brightley."

He blinked as he found himself pulled into a slow dance. "Lucas. Hey." Kace was more than a little surprised to see the red-haired eyeful. It had been months. "What an odd place to run into you."

A bright smile lit his sexy face. His amber eyes sparkled with mischief. "It's a small world."

It seemed so. Lucas was the first and last one-night stand Kace had ever had. He didn't know what to talk about. They hadn't talked much the last time they saw each other. A smile exploded across Kace's face. He fought a laugh. "This is uncomfortable."

"What? You haven't seen everyone here naked?"

Kace's shoulders relaxed. "At least two."

Lucas shook his head. His smile didn't dim. "I'm relieved to see someone I half-ass know."

The comment caught him off guard. "Why are you at the wedding reception of someone you don't know?"

"I know the grooms." He glanced around. "Actually, I know quite a few people, but they're all from work."

Kace nodded. "Have you had dinner? I mean, other than the typical reception food?"

"No. We should definitely remedy that, though."

"Agreed."

Maybe he wouldn't drown tonight after all. He had gone into that one night with Lucas fully understanding it was no more than sex. They had simply been two people looking for the same thing. He didn't need Jamison. Kace had options. He would explore them.

CHAPTER TWO

As MUCH AS JAMISON loved these types of jobs, he had too much time to think. Angie only hired him to help her fall asleep. Then he would place pillows in his place and go. Unfortunately, he couldn't stop thinking about his encounter with Kace.

Angie's husband had passed away a little over a year ago. She had spent months unable to sleep properly after his death. For fifteen years, she had slept in his arms. While Angie could tell her girlfriends about how hard it was to sleep, there was less than zero chance she would find a man who would cuddle with her without the expectation of sex. She wasn't ready for that. In fact, she wasn't sure she would ever be. All of that circled right back to Kace. Fuck that guy. This job mattered. It left him fulfilled. Each time he left Angie with her peacefully sleeping, he felt good about himself. Just because he hadn't needed ten years of college or whatever, that didn't make his job any less important. People died of broken hearts too.

Jamison had spent twenty years in the Army, from the age of eighteen. He had been deployed eight times in those years before he retired. He knew all about stress, feeling helpless, and generally living at his breaking point. Jamison didn't want that any longer. This was a peaceful career. He had been at it for two years and it made him feel good. Sometimes, people wanted to talk. Others just wanted to be held for the sake of human contact. Then there were people like Angie. No matter the client, his life was better now, and he genuinely believed he made other people's lives better too. Fuck. He couldn't stop harping on it.

When Jamison was certain Angie slept, he slipped from the bed and went through his usual routine of moving pillows before sneaking out and locking the door behind him. He waited until he was in his truck to turn on his phone. Jamison always kept the device off while he was with clients. They paid for his full attention and they got it. He had missed a call from an unknown number, a text from his ex, and a text from the same unknown number. Jamison sent the text from his ex straight to the trash without reading it before he opened the other one.

Unknown number: *This is Kace. I got your number from Haven. I didn't want to message you through the app where I hired you, in case anyone else can see those. Anyhow, I owe you a huge apology. I tried to call and tell you myself. You're probably like me and don't answer calls from unknown numbers. I just wanted to say that I hired you because I need you. You're right to feel insulted. Your job is important. Don't worry. I won't bother you again.*

Well, damn. Now he felt bad for storming out of his cousin's wedding reception over this. Sometimes he let his temper get the best of him. This time, it had cost him a moment with his family and a client. That was pretty typical of him. In the end, he was always the one he hurt the most.

With no plan, he saved Kace's number to his phone. Maybe he could still salvage things.

Jamison: *I turn my phone off when I'm with clients. I appreciate your apology. Anytime you need my services, I'm fine to continue working with you. No hard feelings.*

There. Professional. Very adult like. He set his phone aside and started his truck. Before he could back from the driveway, he got a notification. Jamison checked his phone again. He had a job offer waiting. It was only eleven. There was still time to squeeze in another appointment. It was

Kace. He took a steadying breath and hit accept. Jamison had proven he could be professional. Money was money.

On autopilot, he drove to Kace's place. When he arrived at the upscale home deep in an affluent neighborhood, Jamison donned his mental armor. He made it through Afghanistan. This was nothing. He made his way to the door. Barely any light shone inside. The place looked the way it always did when he arrived—like Kace was ready for bed. He rang the doorbell.

Kace answered the way he always did, wearing pajama pants and a T-shirt. "Hey. Thanks for coming." He sounded formal, obviously ready to treat this like the transaction it was. Unfortunately, something strange had happened to his brain since their argument. Jamison didn't see him as a client any longer. Kace knew his real name. They'd danced. Jamison saw his light green eyes and messy dark hair and couldn't stop thinking *he's beautiful*. Jamison was fucked.

It was uncomfortable. They were stiff. He felt exactly like a stranger held him. He made it all of ten minutes.

"I guess I ruined this." He said the words against Jamison's massive chest. Kace couldn't look the guy in the eye.

"What do you think you've ruined?"

He sounded half asleep—like he was the one getting the most from this service. That relaxed Kace's shoulders a bit.

"This arrangement. It doesn't feel the same. I can't relax. Like, do you want me to keep calling you James? Or am I allowed to call you Jamison? This just doesn't feel the same." Things felt intimate and Kace couldn't relax because it shouldn't be intimate.

"Jamison."

He really sounded dead to the world.

Kace leaned back a hair. A smile exploded across his face. Jamison was out. His discomfort disappeared. It was obvious Jamison had no issues with holding Kace. Kace didn't even care the guy was sleeping on the job. He still intended to get his money's worth.

Kace grabbed his phone and set his alarm before using the app on his phone to turn out the lights. He put the device away, grabbed the covers, and settled back down. His mind wouldn't be quiet. When he went to dinner with Lucas, he had hoped his night would end differently. When Lucas had been called into work, Kace definitely hadn't seen the evening going in this direction. He kind of preferred this. Kace liked Lucas. He was some sort of courier for the rich. The guy got paid a lot of money to be ready for anything at all hours of the day. Kace gathered his clientele was small but elite. Like top one percent elite. But there was something about the guy that kept Kace from chasing him. He was too young for Kace, for one thing. He hadn't truly considered that age gap the night they had met purely for sex. Sitting across from the guy at dinner felt different. There was something just slightly disingenuous about him. Jamison didn't feel fake. Kace's mind screeched to a halt. Wait. Why was he thinking about Lucas and Jamison in the same breath? The two very different arrangements. Extremely different. He was being dumb. Jamison was here for the money. He didn't see Kace as anything more than a client and why should he see Kace as more? Kace was just a client. Damn. What was wrong with him... well, Jamison was rather snuggly. There was a reason Kace kept hiring him. Realistically, would he want to be in this position with someone he didn't find attractive? He had to stop. Kace couldn't let his mind travel that path. He had already insulted the poor guy. The last thing he wanted was for Jamison to accuse Kace of thinking he was a whore again. He just needed to fall asleep, put these crazy thoughts behind him, and try again with Lucas. Kace just needed to get laid. That was all. Lucas was too young to have a real relationship with Kace, but he was definitely old enough to be amazing in bed. Kace had needs. Once it was out of his system, this would just be a service provided. That was it.

Jamison shifted in his sleep. Kace found himself half squashed beneath Jamison's massive weight. It was kind of nice. But then Jamison shoved his hand beneath Kace's shirt, as if seeking warmth... or bare skin. Kace realized they were both hard and there was no denying it. The guy's huge erection dug into his hip. Kace closed his eyes and focused on breathing. Jamison was asleep. People couldn't control what they did in their sleep. No big deal. Fuck. He really had to call Lucas.

This was about to be the longest night of his life.

CHAPTER THREE

DARKNESS ENGULFED JAMISON AS he slowly woke. He felt oddly rested for the middle of the night. The more his mind cleared, the more the horror set in. He wasn't home. Jamison had fallen asleep with Kace. Holy shit. That had never happened to him. Normally, he had a terrible time sleeping, so it was easy for him to stay awake with clients. He couldn't believe he had done something so stupid.

Jamison eased his hand in his pocket to find his phone. The last thing he wanted was to disturb Kace. He turned on the device, checked the face, and shot straight up. It was nearly noon. He blinked at his surroundings. Even in the pitch black, he could make out a few things. There was the faintest hint of light streaming in around the curtains and there was a nightlight in the bathroom. The bed was empty. Jamison scrambled from the bed. He felt like a total idiot. It looked like it was his turn to say he was sorry. He couldn't believe this had happened. Jamison rushed from the room, determined to apologize. The house was totally silent. In the kitchen, he found a plate of muffins and a note.

Jamison,

You were sleeping so peacefully, I didn't want to bother you. I made you breakfast. There's orange juice in the fridge and coffee in the pot you can reheat. When you're ready, just lock the door behind you. No need to rush. I know I can trust you. Just text me when you leave so I can set the alarm on the app. Thanks for a great night of sleep.

Well, shit. He could hardly charge Kace for this. Jamison checked the app on his phone to withdraw the invoice. It had already been paid. He tried issuing a refund, but it was rejected. It seemed the app was being a bitch. He obviously couldn't win.

Jamison eyed the muffins. They looked good. Surely, it would be rude if he didn't eat at least one. He picked a small one and broke off a piece. A hum of delight rose in his throat. Banana nut. His favorite. It even had the little streusel topping on top he loved. He ate as he moved to the fridge. Just like Kace said, a full container of orange juice was inside. It was freshly squeezed. Jesus. Jamison was falling in love. His stomach was the way to his heart. After finding the glassware and pouring a cup, he pulled out a stool at the counter and sat. While he ate his second muffin, he tried again to refund Kace's money. It just wouldn't go through. With a huff, he started on a third muffin. It was like he was doomed to wreck things with Kace. He supposed they were even now, but he still needed to apologize.

Jamison eyed the nearly empty plate. Kace had said he made Jamison breakfast—like he cooked. That didn't sound like someone angry. He wondered what brand muffin mix this was. Damn. It was good. Jamison looked around for the trash can. He wasn't above checking. When he pushed the lever down with his foot and the lid popped up, he froze. Banana peels and eggshells stared up at him. Goddamn. He had made the muffins from scratch. That was it. Jamison had to marry him. He chuckled at his thoughts. Jamison hadn't felt this good in a long time. It was amazing what a solid night of sleep did for him. Now he needed a shower. Regretfully, he left the final two muffins behind. While he wanted them, he didn't want to wipe Kace out. It was possible Kace expected to eat at least one when he got home. He rinsed his glass and put it in the dishwasher before heading back to the bedroom to make the bed. After a quick trip to the bathroom, he was out. The minute he climbed into his truck, he texted Kace. He didn't want to drive away, leaving Kace's house without the alarm set.

Jamison: *I'm incredibly sorry. This has never happened to me before. Not once have I fallen asleep on a client. I tried refunding your money, but I guess something is wrong with the payment app. It keeps rejecting the refund. Let me know if there's a different way I can send the money. Or if you'd like, my next session is free. That is, if you're still willing to work with me. I feel terrible. Thank you for breakfast. It was terrific. I'm out now if you want to secure things. Again, so sorry.*

To his surprise, his phone almost immediately chirped.

Kace: *It could've happened to anyone. You don't owe me a thing. I slept great.*

Fuck. Jamison really had to hang on to Kace. He chewed his bottom lip. Oddly, he didn't want their conversation to end, but he couldn't think of anything else to say. So he just typed.

Jamison: *Still, seriously, let me know about that free session. I can't have you out here dissatisfied.*

The moment he hit send, he felt dumb. Was he flirting? Surely it didn't sound that way. Did it? What was wrong with him? That didn't explain why he hadn't even started his truck. He sat staring at his phone with his breath held, waiting for a response. Jamison watched the three dots jump, showing Kace typing. They kept disappearing before reappearing. Jamison thought his nerves might snap. He nearly sighed when the text finally appeared.

Kace: *Actually, I'm very much the opposite of dissatisfied. At the risk of sounding like I'm trying to be that guy, I'd kind of like to do it again. I get that's something you don't do, and I swear I'm not trying to insult you. No doubt I'll regret hitting send on this text, but I woke up feeling great this morning. Maybe this is a new service you could offer? I don't know what I'm trying to say. Feel free to ignore this text. Last night was nice.*

Jamison chewed on the side of his nail and read the text three times. Kace didn't say anything in particular that led Jamison to suspect Kace was trying for more than another peaceful night of sleep. Still, he felt a vibration between the lines.

Maybe it was wishful thinking. Possibly, he could just push a little more.

Jamison: *What time do you get off work? My calendar is free tonight. Maybe we can get dinner and work out the details or something.*

God, he sounded like an idiot.

Kace: *I'm off at sex. Maybe I could cook you dinner...*

Kace: *Six. I meant six. Autocorrect always getting the best of me at the worst times.*

Jamison couldn't stop smiling. His stomach growled like he hadn't just eaten a full plate of muffins. Kace was obviously a kick-ass chef and Jamison was a man who loved to eat. Plus, he wanted this.

Jamison: *Sounds great. What time? Seven? Six thirty? I could help cook. Or at least bring whatever you need.*

Kace: *Seven. That gives me time to shower. Hospital germs and all that. Just bring yourself. I've got the rest.*

He was phenomenal. Jamison was likely seeing things that weren't there, but Dr. Kace Brightley was also sexy. He would see where this went and try not to read too much into things.

Jamison: *See you then.*

Kace*: Yeah. See you.*

Damn. It was too late. He read all the way into things and he liked what he saw.

Kace spent the day trying not to over-think. He also worked double time to get out of work a few minutes early. While he wasn't a hundred percent sure what was happening, tonight felt a hell of a lot like a date. He hated to hope, though. Life rarely went his way when it came to his personal life. No doubt this wouldn't be any different. Still, when the doorbell rang, Kace wiped his sweaty palms on his thighs like a high school kid about to make it to second base for the first time. He was in so much trouble.

When he opened the door, hunger struck. Jamison stood on the other side with his overnight bag and flowers. He was all smiles and taking up too much space. Kace was ridiculously happy to see him.

Jamison shook the flowers a little. "I didn't know what to contribute, so I brought these."

Kace relieved him of them. "They're beautiful. You can put your bag in the bedroom, if you'd like."

Jamison stepped inside.

Kace closed the door behind him. "I didn't think to ask if you're allergic to anything or if you're a vegetarian."

"Nah. None of that. Something smells good." Without waiting for a response, he headed down the hall.

Kace returned to the kitchen. He found a vase for the flowers and tried not to read too much into things. The last thing Kace wanted was to assume anything and get hurt. Jamison was a good-looking man. That was all. So he had crushed Kace beneath him with his massive dick, pinning Kace to the bed. That could happen to anyone. It likely would have been the same, no matter who Jamison had fallen asleep with. Kace wasn't special.

"So, is there anything I can help you do?"

Kace nearly jumped out of his skin when Jamison appeared behind him. He wasn't used to there being a second person in the house. He tried to hide his overreaction by donning a bright smile.

"No. It's good. You're a guest. Just find a seat. It won't be long."

Jamison looked unsure. It was obvious he wasn't used to being useless. He moved to the island and sat. He picked up a Ziplock with two muffins. "You didn't eat them."

"I made them for you. You can take them home." He set the flowers in the center of the island. When he glanced Jamison's way, Jamison had a line between his eyebrows. "What's wrong? If you didn't like them, you don't have to take them. I just didn't want them to go to waste if you wanted them. But I won't be offended if you didn't care for them. I didn't know what to make for you this morning since I didn't know how long you'd sleep. Muffins was something I knew would stay good."

"They were delicious. I had to make myself stop eating them so I'd leave some for you. But why did you make something you didn't want?"

Kace shrugged. It hadn't been a big deal. Cooking soothed him. It was very predictable. As long as he followed the same recipe, he always got the same results. Life was rarely like that. "I like to cook, and I figured you'd be hungry. I ate a banana while they baked."

"Why are you single?"

A smile snapped to Kace's lips. He genuinely liked Jamison. "I work all the time, my schedule is all over the place, and I'm boring. When I'm off work, I just want to relax, and love won't just fall in my lap—I'm guessing. I'll keep trying, though, because I'm not about to actually go out looking for it."

Jamison's smile kept Kace from feeling dumb over his confessions.

Still, he had to move on. "What about you? I never thought to ask if you're single or even if the cuddling is your only job. It seems like I should know those things."

"Since I'm currently having dinner with you, you can rest assured I'm single. I'm too busy to cheat. Cuddling is my only job. I came home from Afghanistan technically disabled and incapable of holding a normal job. In both cases, dating and employment, no one wants someone who might fall into a PTSD-ridden mess at any moment."

This was a date. Kace heard the rest too, but if Jamison thought being here would be cheating with anyone else, then that meant date, right? *Gah*. He was a disaster.

He had to say something before Jamison thought he had been scared off by the confessions. "Well, I'm a doctor. I'm equipped to handle a PTSD-ridden mess, so you're good."

Jamison's sweet smile warmed Kace's heart. Obviously, he had said the right thing. That felt rare lately. A timer went off, pulling him from the moment of holding Jamison's gorgeous stare. Kace focused on pulling things out of the oven. He had no clue where this night was headed, but couldn't wait to find out.

There were bursts when Jamison wondered if Kace was nervous. He imagined it took a lot of confidence to be a doctor, so maybe not. While Jamison usually prided himself on his ability to read people, Kace was different. He had taken a hell of a risk by saying being there would be cheating if he wasn't single. If Kace had corrected him, it would have been a hell of a test to his shamelessness. Kace hadn't said he was wrong, so that was one less thing on his mind.

Dinner had been every bit as amazing as breakfast. He loaded the dishwasher. Jamison swore—beyond the taste—he didn't recall much about eating or cleaning up afterward. They never moved from each other's sides or stopped talking. For the life of him, he couldn't understand now why he had been even the slightest bit bothered by anything Kace said at the reception. Kace could be a little awkward and it was adorable.

If Jamison had realized that sooner, he would have handled things differently. Then again, if he had, then maybe he wouldn't be here right now. He would still just be taking jobs with Kace, cuddling and nothing more. Jamison would never have known how much he missed.

"We've been talking so much; we haven't really talked about you staying the night."

Yeah. Jamison had purposely steered clear of that topic. He didn't want things to turn businesslike and ruin the night.

Kace shifted from foot to foot and twisted his fingers. It was on display now. Kace was nervous. "I mean, are you going to send me an invoice? Are you here because you want to be? I don't even know what I'm trying to say. I guess I just don't want to assume."

Jamison closed the dishwasher. "Yeah, about that." He snagged Kace's waist and pulled him in for a kiss. At first, Kace was stiff in his arms, as if shocked by the move. Then he felt Kace melt as their tongues met. It was obvious it was their first kiss. For a moment, things were slightly awkward. Then Jamison realized he had backed Kace against the counter, and the air heated.

"So that's a no on the invoice?"

A laugh burst from Jamison at Kace's breathless words. "Yeah. I'll be pretty upset if you try to pay me."

"Good." Kace dragged Jamison back down for another kiss. This time, Kace obviously felt a little better prepared. He made Jamison moan. It was a completely involuntary sound. The way Kace curled his tongue around Jamison's and then bit his bottom lip, before sucking. Whoa. He was invested.

"Dessert or bed?"

Jamison grabbed two handfuls of ass and lifted. When Kace wrapped his legs around Jamison, he headed down the hall while still trying to steal any kisses he could get. In no time, he had Kace beneath him. They made out like teens for what felt like forever before clothes finally started to disappear.

"Tell me how you want it."

Kace's fingertips dug into Jamison's back when Jamison growled the words against his throat. "I want you inside me."

Fuck yeah. He was in. Jamison wasted no time ripping into his wallet to find a condom while Kace dove for the bedside table, searching for the lube. When he found it, Jamison was already suited up. That was how ready he was to go. He grabbed the bottle from Kace. Jamison wanted to make sure Kace was as wet and ready as possible. There was a genuine concern he might hurt the guy. Jamison wasn't unaware of his size. He was proportionate all over, and it wasn't always a good thing. More than once, men hadn't come back for seconds. He honestly liked Kace. They had to do this again. That meant taking his time, except Kace wasn't having it.

Jamison ended up on his back with Kace fully in charge, with no clue how it happened. One second, he had been ready to get to work wetting Kace. The next, Kace straddled his body with his head thrown back. He took Jamison like he had waited his whole life for Jamison's package. Jamison's eyes burned from not blinking. He couldn't look away. Not only was Kace beautiful, he was also arousing as fuck. He was like a whole-ass porno. The guy didn't hide his desire or enjoyment. He openly took what he wanted. Jamison hadn't expected to only be along for the ride—or to just be the ride. Yet here he was, and he wasn't mad about it. He couldn't stop stroking Kace so he could get the full show. Jamison wanted to watch him come unglued. He was turned on, desperate, and terrified he wouldn't last much longer. Kace was a lot. He had Jamison feeling all the things. Then Kace caught him totally off guard by blowing much faster than Jamison expected. All Jamison could do was gasp and hang on as Kace's body tried sucking him dry. He went from watching the show to whining his way through the most powerful orgasm he had ever experienced. Jamison couldn't breathe. He heard the needy, desperate sounds escaping him and he couldn't stop. His entire body shook as he tried getting deeper into Kace's ass. He had a bad feeling he used Kace like a rag doll as he lost control. Jamison couldn't temper his strength. He had Kace by the hips, lifting him and dragging him back down while slamming his hips upward, taking Kace as hard as possible. The fight to pull every twitch and drop of cum from his body was real. Every second was carnal. Then nothing but wheezed and ragged breathing filled the air as Kace collapsed across his chest.

Jamison fought like hell to grab a single full thought and hang on. "Holy shit."

He felt Kace chuckle against his chest.

Jamison held him tighter. "I'm not joking. Holy shit."

Kace laughed harder.

"What the fuck was that? Why can't I think straight?" Jamison couldn't stop. No one had ever snatched his soul before. He had heard people say that, but always laughed about it. Now someone had rocked him to his core and Jamison still couldn't breathe. He wanted to do it again.

"I've never been this angry with myself for only having the one condom."

A wheezed laugh cut through the air. "Take mercy on me. I'm not exactly young."

The comment struck Jamison. This guy had just flipped his world upside down and Jamison honestly had no idea how old he was. He didn't know Kace's middle name or if he had any siblings. Jamison wanted to know all those things. He wanted everything. The truth slowly dawned. He had met the one. Now he just had to convince Kace he was worth keeping.

CHAPTER FOUR

EVERY FEW MINUTES, KACE caught himself smiling like an idiot. He would force the senseless grin away, only to catch himself again. He didn't know if or when he would see Jamison again, but he had high hopes. His entire body sang with happiness. He had fallen asleep in some very sexy arms and woken to a delicious mouth kissing its way down his body. Fuck. He was in trouble. Not because he didn't want a relationship or anything, but because he wanted this so fucking badly, he could taste it. If they didn't talk again, he would be crushed.

Kace had always preferred the night shift. It allowed him to sleep in and get errands done without rushing. Tonight, he resented working at all. When he had left for his shift, he had welcomed the distraction. Jamison had an appointment. Kace over thought their every second together. He needed to keep busy to hold his focus, except it wasn't happening. Kace still couldn't stop questioning what this was, which was incredibly dumb. He knew better than to expect anything from anyone these days. Everyone was just hopping from one bed to the next. No one wanted anything real. He wasn't special. Fuck, though. Jamison had made him feel like no one else has ever fucked him so good. The pride that guy had made him feel, damn. Kace didn't know if he would survive, knowing it was a one-night stand. If he never heard from Jamison again, he would spend the rest of his life second-guessing himself. Hell, there was a very real possibility Jamison was a huge player who simply had his act down to perfection. He wouldn't be the first guy to completely fuck with Kace's head. Kace wanted to believe, though. He was at a place in his life where he desperately wanted something real.

Kace hadn't been joking last night. He had no intention of going out and searching for love. It would have to fall from the sky. The dating scene was complete trash. He wouldn't disturb his peace with that dumpster fire. Kace would rather be alone, and that said a lot, because he was lonely. That was sad to admit, but true. Not that loneliness made him desperate. He hadn't fallen on Jamison because he was convenient. The guy was so, so sexy. He was huge, with a hairy chest, and took up way too much space. Jamison would cost a fortune to feed, and he was like a space heater in bed. Kace loved all those things. Those qualities made him real. Jamison wasn't some dude at the club with over-styled hair who rarely left the gym. He wasn't the guy who bleached his teeth and waxed every inch of his body, hoping to be the prettiest boy at the club. Jamison was just a genuine person. He was also so, so nice, and damn it, Kace would be upset if they never spoke again.

A flash of familiar red hair caught Kace's eye and pulled him from his thoughts. He grabbed a bottle of water from the cooler.

As he made his way through the line, he kept his gaze locked on the man's back. He was a good ninety percent sure it was Lucas, three people ahead of him. It just seemed like such a huge coincidence to run into him here. Why was he at the hospital cafeteria? Kace grabbed a salad and chose his dressing while trying not to lose sight of Lucas. He gave up when it came time to pull out his phone to pay. It probably wasn't him. That was just too weird. He grabbed his stuff and turned to find a seat. Lucas stood behind him with a soda and sandwich.

A bright smile lit the guy's face. His amber eyes sparkled with happiness. "Hey. I thought that was you."

Kace automatically smiled. Lucas was pretty irresistible. "Hey. What a crazy place to run into each other."

Lucas shrugged. "I mean, you work here and everyone ends up here eventually."

He guessed that was true. After all, working at the hospital was how he had seen Joesph again after years of no contact.

Lucas motioned toward a nearby table. "Want to sit together?"

It seemed weird not to since they knew each other. "Sure." They moved to the table. Kace spoke while they got settled. "So, is everything okay? People are rarely here for anything good."

"I'm one of the exceptions. My younger sister had a baby. Her husband is currently deployed and won't get here for a couple of days. I'm staying with her."

"That's nice of you."

Lucas shrugged. "She's my sister."

Kace liked the way Lucas made the claim like that mattered. A lot of people had shitty siblings they couldn't stand.

"I really enjoyed dinner the other night. You have no idea how disappointed I was to get called away."

Well, shit. He was uncomfortable. It didn't make sense. One night with Jamison didn't make them a couple. He was under no obligation to reject Lucas. Kace honestly couldn't pinpoint why he suddenly didn't want to flirt. Jamison probably didn't even want anything serious. Damn.

"It was nice, but I get it. Work has to come first sometimes."

"I'd hoped to make you come first."

He didn't know how to untangle himself from this. Possibly, he would be crazy to let someone like Lucas slip through his fingers... again. That thought drew him up short. He had already been down this road with Lucas. Lucas had already proved he wouldn't call. Kace wouldn't risk his shot at something real over someone he knew to be fake.

"Here's the thing. I'm not really looking for a fling at this stage in my life." Damn, he sounded old, but really. Compared to Lucas, he was. The guy deserved to have his fun while he could, but Kace was tired. He didn't want to play games. "You don't strike me as the type to settle down."

Lucas shrugged. "Spend your break with me. You might change your mind."

Jesus. He really was pretty... and skinny. Lucas didn't look like he could keep Kace warm at night. He definitely wasn't pillow material. Kace had hired Jamison for a reason. He loved to cuddle. Kace probably enjoyed being held more than the sex. What was wrong with him? Lucas was a sexy guy. Kace would be crazy to pass up his chance. Why was he always such a mess?

"Hey. Damn. I didn't get here quick enough."

Kace started at Jamison's sudden arrival. He claimed the chair next to Kace like Kace should have expected him.

Jamison passed a food container his way. "Oh, good. You're just having salad. That goes great with lasagna."

Kace was slightly disoriented. "You brought me lasagna?"

"Of course. I can't have you going hungry on the night shift." He looked Lucas' way. "What's up?"

Kace glanced between them. He didn't know what to do or say.

A slight smirk rested on Lucas' face, making things even more confusing. "Jamison."

Fuck. They knew each other, which he supposed made sense. They had both been guests at Joesph's wedding.

Lucas stood. "I need to get back to my sister. It was good seeing you. I'm sure we'll see each other again."

"Yeah." Kace nodded like an idiot while hoping he hadn't blown his chance with both men.

Jamison obviously had zero insecurities. He was all smiles. "Try the lasagna. You cooked for me. It's my turn."

Kace popped the lid on the Tupperware. "How did you even know where and when to find me? Oh, this looks amazing."

Jamison set his arm across the back of Kace's chair. "I knew you worked tonight and guessed you probably had your lunch break about halfway through the night. When I got here, I stopped the first nurse I saw and hit the jackpot. So, just dumb luck, really. Are you having a good night?"

"I am now."

Jamison's bright smile made the claim worthwhile. A happy sigh rang through Kace's head. He was so gorgeous.

Kace took a bite before he made a fool of himself. He was thoroughly distracted. "Wow. This is great. Between the two of us cooking, we'll both be as big as a house by this time next year." Kace kind of wanted to slap himself. He really sounded like he assumed they were a couple.

Jamison's expression turned heated. Kace couldn't look away. The way Jamison watched him through hooded lids had Kace ready to risk it all. "Was that your way of saying you'll keep me?"

Kace went still. He hadn't expected this conversation. "Are you asking?"

"Well, I know that's what I want, but I'll never just assume, and I'll take whatever you're willing to give."

He had no idea how impeccable his timing was, considering Kace had just finished telling Lucas he wanted something real. "I'd be beyond proud to tell people you're mine."

Jamison stole a quick kiss. "Same."

The world vanished around them. Kace forgot where they were. All he saw was Jamison. "I get off at midnight. Is that too late for you?"

Jamison shook his head. "I have an appointment at ten. So I'll probably be done just in time to tuck you into bed."

"I'd love that."

Jamison kissed him again. "Then it's a date. Now eat your dinner. You'll need your strength."

Kace's face hurt from smiling. He had no idea if they would last, but he definitely wanted to find out. Kace had a bad feeling this was about to be the longest shift of his life. Midnight couldn't come fast enough.

Jamison had taken a risk by showing up at Kace's job. All day, he had over thought things and driven himself crazy. Finally, he'd broken. He had to know where they stood. If Kace wanted them to be a one-night thing, or just friends with benefits, Jamison needed to know now before he got invested. Jamison was definitely the type to have expectations. He was too old to play games. Even though he realized he was a bit of a headcase, and his job probably made him a little undesirable as far as relationship material, Jamison wanted something real. He wasn't above accepting whatever Kace offered. Still, he wanted to go into things with his eyes open. Kace, saying he wanted to keep Jamison, felt a lot like winning the lottery. He honestly hadn't expected that outcome. Lucas being there also hadn't been on his bingo card. He would look into that too.

Thankfully, Kace chatted happily, keeping Jamison from accidentally admitting how he had paced all day.

"You're beautiful." Jamison truly hadn't meant to cut Kace off mid-sentence like that. He also didn't want to admit he hadn't heard a word Kace said. Kace was gorgeous, and it was distracting. It didn't help matters that Jamison couldn't get past how hot their night together had been. He was obsessed.

Kace chuckled. "Thank you. The feeling is mutual."

"That's not really a compliment I usually get."

Kace looked taken aback. "Seriously? People literally see your photo and then hire you to come hold them. I'd think that would be a dead giveaway that you're sexy."

Jamison blinked. Surely that wasn't true. "People pick me because I'm very pillow-like."

A laugh burst from Kace. Even as surprised as it sounded, it was still hot. He snagged the collar of Jamison's shirt and hauled him in for a kiss. "You're adorable and people are vain." A buzz had Kace pulling away and digging into the pocket of his doctor's coat. He came out with a pager. "Damn. I have to go." His gaze shot to his food. He looked sad to leave it behind.

"Go. I'll pack this up and make sure you get it later."

"You're amazing."

Jamison swiped a kiss across his lips. "I've got you. Now get back to work."

With a sad-sounding sigh, Kace stood. "I'll see you in a few hours."

Jamison watched him go. Between the scrubs and his walk, Kace screamed confidence. He just looked like a guy who could save lives. Jamison bit his bottom lip. Damn. That was really his. When Kace disappeared from sight, Jamison gathered the food. He would make sure Kace ate before bed. It was his job now to take care of him, and he would. As he headed in the direction of the parking garage, he spotted Lucas. The guy was leaned against the wall, almost as if he had been waiting for Jamison. That suspicion doubled when Lucas straightened when he saw Jamison.

The guy's smirk always made Jamison want to punch him. He always brought out the worst in Jamison. "So, since when do you have a sister?"

An evil-sounding chuckle rumbled from Lucas. "Since it suited my needs. Since when do you cook?"

It was Jamison's turn to smirk. "That's nothing new. You were just unworthy."

Lucas' condescending smile never budged. "Ouch. That's big talk from someone who's too big of a mess to keep a job. I guess that would give you plenty of time to cook."

"It's always fun running into you. Stay away from Kace."

Lucas went back to leaning against the wall. "I think I'll let him tell me to go away." His eyes flashed with a familiar sexual promise. "So far, he hasn't."

Jamison snorted before he could stop himself. "Yeah. If that's all you have to offer, and it is, I'm not worried. A guy like Kace would never choose trash like you." He took a step closer, intimidating Lucas with his size, something he hated doing. In this case, it was necessary. "If he gets hurt because of your bullshit, you'll wish this shady-ass job had gotten you killed."

A deadly chuckle that got all the way beneath Jamison's skin fell from Lucas' lips. His expression turned deadly—just like the man. Now they were getting real. "No one would dare fucking cross me like that. Everyone knows what happens to anyone who fucks with mine. You should heed that warning. When people threaten me, they usually disappear. I'm only entertaining you because we have history and you're fun. Don't mistake my kindness for weakness. That's how people end up dead."

"Kace deserves better."

Lucas rolled his eyes. Jamison hated that he still thought the guy was hot. He shouldn't. Lucas was nothing but trouble. "Don't worry, squishy. I'm not here for him." Lucas' gaze flickered over Jamison's shoulder. Lucas' stance changed. His jacket shifted and Jamison caught sight of the gun he carried. His eyes never shifted from whoever headed their way. Jamison watched Lucas turn into the weapon he had been hired to be. "You should definitely move along." His gaze flickered Jamison's way for half a second. "You don't want to be here."

An aggravated growl rose in Jamison's throat. He didn't argue. Jamison walked away without another word. Lucas was right. Jamison didn't want to play witness to the underbelly of the world. He didn't want to hear Lucas call him squishy the way he used to do—only for it to be bull-shit. Jamison had done his time and now he wanted a soft life. Jamison wanted a good man to give him pet names. He hat-ed how many times he had fallen into Lucas' bullshit, simply because he des-perately wanted something real. Jamison genuinely believed Kace was different. They might be exactly what he searched for, and he was dead serious. He would make Lucas regret being born if he didn't stay away from Kace.

CHAPTER FIVE

JAMISON STARED AT THE ceiling and tried to relax. He couldn't stop thinking about his run-in with Lucas. Time wouldn't move its ass so he could get to Kace. He had a bad feeling his vibe was the reason Angie still wasn't asleep.

"I'm sorry. You probably have other appointments to get to."

Jamison pulled his attention back to the person paying him to be there. "You're fine. Don't worry about me."

Angie shifted positions, as if giving up on actual sleep. "It's my wedding anniversary. I doubt I'll get any rest."

Jamison's heart twisted. "I'm so sorry. You should've said something sooner."

He felt Angie shrug. "It doesn't matter. I'm just too in my thoughts to relax. Can we talk about something else to busy my mind? I know you probably don't talk about yourself for safety reasons. It's okay if you want to dodge my questions. I just don't know that much about you."

He wasn't worried about Angie. Most people he wouldn't tell anything, but she was just trying to survive. "What would you like to know?"

"Anything you're willing to disclose, I suppose. Is this your only job? Are you married? Dating? How do they feel about this job? Pick a topic."

Jamison smiled into the dark at being given the opportunity to talk about Kace. "This is my only job. I'm not married, but I am dating someone. He's a doctor." It was crazy how much that filled him with pride. It shouldn't. Being a doctor was just Kace's job, and they'd argued over Jamison telling him that didn't make him special. But it kind of did because Kace actually cared about people. Still, Jamison felt like he needed to add to that statement, so it didn't seem like that was why he wanted the guy. "His job makes it easier for him to understand mine. He knows all the scientific evidence behind what I do."

"I'm glad to hear the passion in your voice when you talk about doing this. It makes me feel better about spending money just to be held."

He hated when he heard shame in people's tone when they talked about hiring him. "You shouldn't feel bad about it at all. You're looking after your health. Sleep is one of the most important keys to staying alive. It affects everything. You shouldn't feel any differently about this than you would a day at the spa. You're protecting your mental wellbeing."

Angie didn't respond. He tilted his head to see her face. She was asleep. He fought a chuckle. Jamison should talk more often. He had bored her to sleep.

Jamison waited another half an hour before going through the usual routine. He should have known there was something unusual about tonight. Angie didn't normally book his services this close together. He hoped she stayed asleep and found the peace she needed. Before he got on the road, he texted Kace.

Jamison: *I'm headed that way. Do you need me to pick up anything?*

Kace: *Nope. I'm good. Thank you for leaving my dinner. That was a nice surprise.*

Jamison: *Of course. I told you I'd take care of it.*

To be honest, Jamison was beyond relieved Kace wasn't angry to see Jamison had been inside his house. Kace was one of the many clients he had the entry codes to their home, and Kace had given him the alarm code this morning, in case he ever wanted to sleep in again. Many times, customers had him locking up their homes and whatnot when they fell asleep. It wasn't like him to abuse that trust, but he had wanted Kace to eat.

Kace: *So you did. See you soon.*

Jamison didn't waste time responding. He wanted to get to Kace's place and try for another taste. Jamison had barely thought of anything else all day. Waking up next to Kace had been pretty fucking amazing too. Things felt real. It had been a long time since he felt this happy and at peace. Kace was the first instance in too long to recall since he'd dared be selfish. He wanted more. Kace made him greedy. Now Jamison needed to see if he could make Kace feel the same.

The second half of his night crawled, exhausting Kace. But knowing Jamison was on his way changed everything. He practically bounced with energy. When the doorbell finally rang, Kace had to take a breath to hide his excitement. He pulled the door open, and Jamison was on him like he had just come home from war. His mouth and hands were everywhere. He kicked the door closed behind him. Kace's feet left the floor. Jamison still tried stealing kisses as he made his way down the hall. Kace was on fire. When he found himself beneath Jamison, he had never felt so desired.

"I can slow down. I've just thought about you too much today."

"We can slow down later."

A wicked-sounding chuckle vibrated against his throat as Jamison kissed it. "Good." His hand shoved inside the front of Kace's pajama pants.

Kace fought a moan. Jamison didn't hold back. He acted like a man bent on making Kace come. Kace kept lifting his hips, trying to fuck Jamison's hand. The desperation was real.

"Please. Damn, Jamison. I want you inside of me when I come."

Jamison moved to his knees and dug both hands in his pockets. A loud bark of laughter burst from Kace when he came out with two handfuls of condoms.

"I'll be damned if I get caught with only one again." He dumped them on the bed-side table and grabbed the lube.

Kace scrambled from his clothes. He wouldn't miss another night of this. Kace knew too well how quickly things could end, leaving him with nothing but the memories. So he would make as many as he could. Kace watched through hooded eyes as Jamison did all the work until he slowly pressed against the tight ring of muscles surrounding Kace's asshole. He was completely relaxed. Kace was guilty of loving a fat cock. He might be a little spoiled by toys and years of being alone. Jamison was so much better.

"That's it. You're so good at taking it."

Kace moaned. He wanted more. Jamison gave it to him. Kace was more than full and he was hooked.

"Yes. Mhmm."

At his encouragement, Jamison stopped taking it easy on him. He folded Kace like a pretzel and fucked him. Kace kept gasping for air and straining toward release. He knew words and sounds left his lips, but his mind stayed completely focused on his goal.

"You have to come for me, Kace. You're not like anyone else. I'm not used to getting to have my way. I won't make it much longer."

At Jamison's claim, Kace worked twice as hard to blow. When he did, he swore his soul left his body. For a moment, he hovered in heaven before returning to life.

Jamison roared as he came. The sound and sight seared its way into Kace's brain. He could easily fall in love with this life. It seemed too good to be true.

Jamison collapsed but kept his weight on his elbows so he wouldn't squish Kace. "Fuck, Kace. You're amazing. What are you doing for the rest of your life?"

A laugh burst from Kace.

Jamison kissed him, smothering the sound. Kace had a hard time not smiling through their kiss. Jamison pulled away.

"Okay. How about tomorrow? What hours do you work?"

"I'm off tomorrow."

"Thank fuck." Jamison claimed his mouth again and Kace let himself dream. This could be real—like, really real. Kace wanted that. He would put the work in. Jamison would see. They would be great. That was a vow.

Chapter Six

JAMISON: *WHAT TIME ARE you taking your lunch break tonight?*

Kace: *Around nine.*

Jamison: *I'll be there with food in tow.*

Kace: *Nice. I can't wait.*

Jamison: *See you soon.*

Kace: *What are your plans for Thanks-giving?*

Jamison: *Haven invited me to dinner, but I haven't said if I'd go yet. I was kind of waiting to see what you have planned.*

Kace: *Would you like to meet my mom? She always cooks.*

Jamison: *I'd love that.*

Kace: *Mom wants you to come for Christ-mas.*

Jamison: *You sure? I think she immediately hated me at Thanksgiving.*

Kace: *LOL! Maybe. Once she realized you were in the military, that changed her mind. She doesn't think anyone is good enough for me. Don't worry. I like you.*

Jamison: *Picture me grumbling under my breath because I am, but it's good. I'm in. Also, maybe we could start a tradition for us. You know I don't have anywhere to go other than Haven's house. Maybe we can do a Christmas Eve or Christmas day thing on the regular—just us.*

Kace: *I love that idea.*

Jamison: *Do you want to go Christmas shopping? I need help to pick out presents.*

Kace: *I'd love to.*

Jamison: *You get off at four, right?*

Kace: *Yep.*

Jamison: *I'll pick you up at five thirty. We can find someplace to eat afterward.*

Kace: *Can't wait.*

Every time Jamison thought about it, he couldn't believe they had been strong and steady for five months. It had been the best months of his life. Even fighting through the packed store with rabid Christmas shoppers didn't dim the happiness he felt simply being with Kace. Kace seemed a little distracted, though.

"Are you good?"

Kace looked his way at the question and flashed a small smile. "Of course. I'm with you."

Jamison wasn't appeased. "Are you sure? You don't sound like you're good."

Kace's smile grew. He shook his head. "Seriously, it's nothing."

It was definitely something. Jamison didn't know if he should keep pushing. Unfortunately, his anxiety wouldn't let it go. "You can talk to me about anything. You know that, right?"

Kace had been hugging his arm for ten minutes while Jamison shopped. He squeezed it harder. "I'm not trying to ruin a nice night out."

Damn. "You have to tell me now. Otherwise, I'll get in my head and convince myself you plan to dump me."

The sweetest expression Jamison has ever seen crossed Kace's features. "Why would you think that? I love you."

Jamison stopped walking, forcing people to flood past them like a boulder in the center of a river. "What? Wait. You've never said that before."

Jamison wished he hadn't had such an over-the-top reaction when Kace looked uncomfortable. "You can forget I said it, if you want. I didn't mean to upset you. It's okay if you don't feel the same. I shouldn't have said anything."

"Kace. Stop talking."

Kace visibly snapped his mouth closed at Jamison's command. He looked crestfallen and Jamison was an idiot. Jamison had to fix things. "I'm a huge dumbass. You just caught me off guard. Of course, I love you too. I don't know why I haven't said it."

A smile exploded across Kace's face. "Probably for the same reason I haven't—because you hadn't."

All Jamison could do was shake his head while he beamed like a fool. "We always have to do things the hard way, don't we?"

"It seems so."

He kissed Kace's forehead and resumed walking. "Don't think you've distracted me, though. What has you in a bad mood?"

"It's ridiculous, and I'd rather not say."

Jamison released a loud and put-upon sigh. "There's not a single thing you can't talk to me about. Even if you think it's idiotic, it's obviously bothering you. I want to hear it."

"All right. Just remember, I already said it's dumb for me to be bothered. My mom called today to tell me we're invited to my cousin's wedding. He's twenty-seven. I'm forty-two and watching everyone tie the knot and settle down. I guess I just thought I'd be in a different place by this age. Everything else I set out to do, I've done, so feeling down about this doesn't make sense. I have a great career. It's one I worked damn hard to get. Obviously, I'm dating an amazing guy. Forget it. Saying everything out loud now makes me sound like a fool."

"No. I get it." He really did. "I'm forty and I feel the same way. When I left the military, I genuinely thought I would walk straight into a picture-perfect life." He flashed Kace a sad smile. "Instead, I came home a PTSD-ridden mess who can't work a normal job or keep anyone because of my job or my crazy. Honestly, every time I see you, I expect you to tell me it's over. If roles were reversed, I don't know that I could handle knowing you're cuddling other people."

Kace leaned his way and kissed his shoulder. "It's not sexual. I know that. Plus, I trust you."

He was wonderful. Jamison spotted a small red teddy bear in green Christmas-themed overalls. He grabbed it and made a show of giving it to Kace. "You should marry me."

Kace's fingers had just closed around the bear when Jamison's impulsive statement landed. He froze. They both still held the bear. Kace blinked like Jamison had snapped his brain.

"Are you being serious?"

Was he? "Yeah." His mouth just kept saying things.

"We've only been together five months."

"Yeah. They've been the best months of my life."

"We literally just admitted to loving each other."

Jamison shrugged. "I've known for a while. Are you saying no?"

"No. I'm not saying no. I'm just waiting for you to realize what you just did."

That was fair. Jamison definitely hadn't expected this. "No need. I did what I did and said what I said."

"Then, yes."

A smile slowly stretched Jamison's lips as the truth sank in. Kace had agreed to marry him. Never in a million years would he have seen that coming. It might have been a surprise, even to him, but Jamison couldn't be happier.

Kace stayed locked in a state of shock through shopping and dinner. He still couldn't decide if Jamison had proposed out of a desire to marry him or be-cause Kace complained about not being married. Kace might have continued his downward spiral of overthinking if Jamison didn't drive straight to the mall after they ate.

"Do you have more gifts to buy?"

"I guess, technically, yeah. They have a jewelry store. Let's get an engagement ring." Jamison climbed from the truck without waiting for Kace to respond.

Kace was right behind him.

Jamison waited with his hand held out for Kace to hold.

Kace didn't say a word. If Jamison was serious, then Kace was too. His parents had gotten married after a month of dating and stayed married until his dad passed away from lung cancer. So far, his mom showed no interest in remarrying. He wanted that. Obviously not the passing away part. But he desperately craved the love and confidence in that love that it took to be bold. If he took a chance on anyone, it would be Jamison.

"Maybe I should wait and get you something nicer than a ring from a chain store. Don't they say one month's salary or some shit? I could probably save that."

Kace heard the embarrassment in Jamison's tone. Neither of them were rich, especially in the terrible economy. He could make real bank if he went into plastic surgery, which he had thought about. That was neither here nor there, though. He had a good job with above average pay, but he also understood living paycheck to paycheck. He had definitely done that throughout college. "That's not what I want. I want you. It's not the ring. It's what it stands for."

Jamison kissed their joined hands. Then life turned surreal again as they moved from case to case while a salesperson made suggestions based on Kace's skin tone. Jamison made sure he never saw a price tag. He was adorable in how seriously he took the matter. Kace couldn't stop staring at him with stars in his eyes. He had no clue how he had gotten so lucky.

Kace narrowed his selection down to three. Jamison shooed him away so he could make the final choice. Kace wandered around the store, eyeing the jewelry. He should get Jamison a necklace for Christmas.

"Are you ready?"

Kace tore his gaze away from the display. "Yeah."

Again, they linked fingers and headed out. "Since you don't work tomorrow, would you like to stay at my place tonight? I could make you breakfast for once."

"You could do that at my place anytime you want, but sure."

Jamison smiled.

Kace tried not to focus on the fact that Jamison hadn't given him the ring. The negative thoughts tried creeping in again. Maybe he had changed his mind.

They rode to Jamison's house with the music loud. They sang along and Kace tried to push all the destructive thoughts from his head. No matter what, he had a great life. He couldn't and wouldn't complain. Jamison was every bit as goofy as him. Neither of them could sing, but they tried and didn't laugh at each other. Since they started dating, Kace's life had been... easy. He didn't know how else to describe the way Jamison's calm demeanor just soothed something in his soul that made everything feel so damn simple.

At Jamison's place—a small rental at the edge of town—Jamison rushed to help him from the truck before grabbing all their shopping bags. Kace shook his head at the way Jamison acted, like he was helpless. While Jamison stuffed gifts in the closet, Kace hit the bathroom. Since they were always at each other's houses, Kace had a toothbrush, and a pair of pajamas pants stashed in there. Kace ran through his nightly routine, getting ready for bed. They probably still had a couple of hours of unwinding, but he wanted to be comfortable. When he came out, he found white Christmas lights tossed everywhere in an obvious rush, creating a romantic glow in the darkness. Jamison waited on one knee.

A smile exploded across Kace's face.

"Will you marry me?"

"I've already said yes, but it's still yes."

With a laugh, Jamison pushed to his feet. He put the ring on Kace's finger. "I wanted to propose properly and give you another chance to change your mind."

Kace didn't bother arguing about how the answer would always be yes. He dove straight into the kiss he wanted to seal the deal. They would always be happy. Kace would make damn sure of that.

CHAPTER SEVEN

IT WAS SO DAMN easy to sleep like the dead with Jamison holding him—no matter where they slept. It took entirely too much shouting and banging to pull Kace from his dreams. Eventually, the violent sounds penetrated his sleep. The bed was empty. Breaking glass sounded through the house. Kace shot from the bed. He darted toward the sound, expecting to find Jamison fighting with an intruder. Kace skidded to a stop as he reached the living room. His kitchen and living room were one open space. Jamison was in the kitchen area, trashing the place like he tossed a stranger's house. The living room had already been torn to shreds.

"Holy shit! What's going on?"

Jamison whipped around at the question—gun in hand and pointed straight at Kace. His eyes were dead. He wasn't there. "Who are you? Why are you here?"

Kace's pulse pounded louder in his ears. He could barely breathe with his heart racing too fast. Kace held up his hands. Even though he could see the gun had a gun lock on it, Jamison stood in the middle of a kitchen full of knives. Plus, he was twice Kace's size. "Come back to me, Jamison."

"How do you know my name? Who sent you?"

Kace jumped at the screamed questions. He desperately tried to stay calm. "It's Kace, baby. Come back to me."

"Kace?" Jamison turned his head from side to side and squinted as if trying to find Kace in a crowd. "Are you okay? Where are they keeping you?"

"I'm right here, baby. Look at me."

Jamison blinked. Then he blinked again. "Kace." He watched Jamison slowly come back to himself. He looked at his hand and dropped the gun like it was on fire. "Oh, my god. Holy shit. What did I do?" He looked horrified and ready to break down.

Kace rushed to the door and quickly stamped into his shoes. "Don't move, baby." He grabbed Jamison's shoes and hurried to his side. "Put these on." He practically lifted Jamison's feet one foot at a time and dressed him like he would a toddler.

"What did I do?"

The horrified whisper calmed Kace like nothing else could have done. He was accustomed to handling emergencies and mental health crises. That was his forte. "I've got you, baby. You're okay. There's glass everywhere so don't move, all right? Let me clean up."

Jamison stood perfectly still, staring into space as if shocked into a statue like state.

Kace grabbed the broom and swept around him, getting the worst of the glass.

"I could've killed you. This could've been your place."

His voice sounded so broken. "You left me behind safely in bed. It's obvious you never would've hurt me. This is just stuff. It's replaceable."

Jamison walked like a slow zombie toward the living room. He picked up the teddy bear he had given Kace earlier in the night. It was ripped in several places. He dropped to his haunches. "We can't ever get this memory back." Jamison covered his face. His silent despair broke Kace's heart. Kace had gone into this relationship knowing Jamison had episodes. Jamison had warned him several times. It was inevitable for Kace to eventually see one. He couldn't lie and say the experience hadn't scared the absolute shit out of him. Jamison had still recognized his voice. Jamison hadn't forgotten he loved Kace. He loved him enough to immediately come back to him.

Kace set the broom aside and moved to comfort Jamison. He rubbed Jamison's back with one hand while he picked up the bear with the other.

"Luckily, some might say I'm a decent doctor. I feel certain I can fix him. Stitches have always been one of my top ten skills."

Jamison sniffed, making Kace realize he cried.

Some things could wait—like this mess. It would still be there tomorrow. "Come on, gorgeous. Let's get back to bed." He urged Jamison to his feet. "I need to hold you."

Jamison swiped at his eyes. He looked like hell. When they reached the bed, Kace removed the shoes he had just placed on Jamison's feet before tucking him under the covers. He toed off his shoes and joined him. Kace cuddled as closely as possible, trying to squeeze the despair from Jamison.

"It's a good thing we're getting married. We'll still have one set of dishes." Kace tried to infuse as much humor as he could into the statement.

"I can't believe you're talking about still marrying me right now."

Jamison's voice sounded rough—like he had spent hours screaming. "Do you think I'd leave you over something you can't help? If I found out I had cancer tomorrow, would you leave me?"

"No." The way he didn't even hesitate let Kace know he had been right to accept that proposal. "I can't think of anything you could do to lose me."

Kace kissed his chest. "Good. I can't control getting cancer any more than you can control this. We just have to work on it like any other health issue—together."

He heard Jamison swallow. "I could've hurt you." His voice broke.

"The moment I said my name, it broke through. I don't think you'd hurt me."

"There isn't a single gun in this house that doesn't have a gun lock for this very reason. I swear, I would never willingly hurt you."

Kace stroked his stomach, trying to keep him calm. "I know, baby. Everything is fine. Okay? I'm not hurt. Let's just get some sleep, and tomorrow, we can deal with the mess."

"Okay."

A few moments passed in silence.

"I'm scared to go to sleep."

God. The whispered confession was nearly Kace's undoing. He was nowhere near as calm as he pretended and seeing Jamison like this was killing him. His insides shook. Kace had seen his share of mental health struggles that led to explosive outbursts in the ER. It was completely different when it was someone he loved.

"Tell me what you need. I'm right here." Even Kace heard the desperation in his voice. He hated that his caregiver demeanor had broken, but it was Jamison. He was the strong retired military man with the heart of gold. Jamison wasn't supposed to be the one who needed help.

Jamison rolled, tucking Kace beneath him. "I'm so goddamn sorry. You should be tearing into me right now or storming out. You have no idea how fucking sorry I am."

Kace rubbed Jamison's back and held on. No one could see him and be angry. None of this was his fault. "I love you. Don't worry. I'm not going anywhere. Just breathe."

"You should leave me. I had a gun pointed at you."

"Baby, stop. You're mine. I'm not leaving you."

Jamison's mouth found his. When their tongues met, he felt Jamison's muscles relax. Maybe they had this. He thought so.

Jamison was a complete fucking wreck. The moment he realized he had held a gun on Kace, just kept replaying in his head. It didn't matter the weapon had been useless. He couldn't imagine how he would feel if roles were reversed.

Yet Kace was beneath him, tasting like a miracle. The mood in the room shifted along with Jamison. He straddled Kace. Jamison was fully aware he didn't deserve Kace. He had to give him a reason to stay.

Jamison urged Kace's hands above his head and then licked his way down the center of Kace's chest. He stopped to suck his nipples before heading further south. Kace's stomach moved in and out on each panted breath he took. He held on to the headboard as Jamison peeled off his boxers. They had already celebrated their engagement earlier. Kace was likely sore. This wasn't about Jamison. He needed Kace to have a reason to keep him. Jamison needed Kace to remember he could make him fly.

He swirled his tongue around Kace's crown, teasing him. A loud moan filled the air. Jamison swallowed him, taking him all the way down his throat.

"Fuck. Yes."

The desperate-sounding praise kept Jamison going. He licked and sucked while fighting the urge to stretch Kace's asshole. Jamison wanted to ready Kace's body to get fucked. He couldn't do that. Kace had to see him as husband material. Not as a greedy head case who might kill him some night. Damn it. If he had any sense, he would send Kace home. It wasn't fair for Jamison to tie Kace to this for life. The thing was, though, he was too weak to let him go.

Kace's hips lifted, trying to fuck Jamison's mouth. "Please? Oh, God. Please?"

Jamison chuckled around Kace's cock. So impatient. Jamison had no intention of letting Kace come yet.

"Please, baby? I want you to fuck me."

Jamison froze. That hadn't been his plan. He didn't know if he punished himself for scaring Kace, but he didn't want to do anything except this. He didn't deserve to be pleasured. "This is about you, sexy. I can go without."

Kace looked turned on and sexy as hell. The night light from the bathroom high-lighted his features. He looked ready to writhe. "I want you to make me drip with cum."

Yeah. He wasn't that strong. No way would he pass up that chance. Jamison was up the bed, finding the lube in no time.

Still, he felt moved to argue for show. "Are you sure? I don't want to hurt you. I've already been too rough on you tonight."

"Let me decide when you've been too rough. Now get inside me."

Goddamn. "Yes, sir." His earlier episode was all but forgotten. Nothing mattered more than their relationship. Jamison lubed Kace's asshole and stretched him the way he had fought not to do earlier. Kace squirmed and whined beneath his touch. He had Jamison on the edge of disappointing him already when he finally led his dick to Kace's asshole. The moment he pressed his way inside, reality struck him like a truck. This was real. Kace really planned to marry him. He honestly intended for Jamison to be the last person he ever made love to again. The doctor in him never would have asked for no condom sex otherwise. He genuinely loved Jamison. Kace had seen the worst of him and still chose him. He didn't deserve this.

"You're the most amazing person I've ever met. I love you so fucking much."

"Good. The feeling is mutual. Now fuck me like you hate me."

He was in. Whatever Kace needed, Jamison had it. He dug his knees into the mattress and gave his everything. Sweat rolled down his back. His muscles screamed. He tasted blood from trying not to come at the tug on his cock. Jamison had been pretty far over the edge and still he didn't think he had ever been this close to insanity.

He felt Kace tense. Jamison held his breath. Kace's body jerked hard as he nearly broke Jamison's dick when his tight hole convulsed.

"Holy shit! Goddamn." An orgasm roared through him, taking him completely out of reality. In a fever high of ecstasy, he saw the future. It was beautiful.

CHAPTER EIGHT

TURNED OUT THERE WAS no avoiding going to Haven's house for Christmas. It hadn't occurred to Kace, even though it should have, but Haven was pretty much all Jamison had. He had been raised by a single father. At eighteen, they had parted ways when Jamison joined the military. From then on, they never really spoke again. He had no clue why, and Kace didn't want to push.

Seeing him joke with Joesph's husband made him realize he never truly saw Jamison interact with people. In theory, he knew Jamison dealt with people all the time. He had clients. Hell, Kace had been one of those clients once upon a time. This was different, though. He was relaxed. It was nice to see.

Joesph rolled his wheelchair to Kace's side and parked beside him. He followed Kace's gaze. "He looks happy. Haven says he dressed up as Santa for the children's hospital. Did I hear that correctly?"

A smile exploded across Kace's face. "He did." Kace grabbed his phone. "I took pics if you want to see."

"Absolutely." Joesph leaned his way. He laughed as they scrolled through the images. Kace realized he still knew Joesph's scent, and the nostalgia was still there, but there were no feelings attached any longer beyond a deep friendship. Joesph had once been the person he loved most in the world. It was strange.

"When Mom told me you two are dating, I'll admit I thought it might be weird." Joesph kept his gaze locked on Kace's phone as he made the confession.

Guilt set in. "I guess I should've discussed things with you first. Honestly, things just moved so fast."

Joesph looked up and met his stare. His eyes were Jamison's. It was so odd that he never saw Joesph in Jamison. "No. It's good seeing you both smile. Jamison hasn't really done that and meant it in a long time. I'm in the unique position of knowing exactly how wonderful you are, so I know he's won the lottery." That was exactly why Kace had missed Joesph so much after their split. He was just one of those people who uplifted everyone around him. Kace still loved him, but it wasn't the same. It was like reconnecting with his best friend.

"I'm trying hard to take care of him."

"What are you two over here looking so intense about?"

Joesph looked away and smiled brightly at his husband's arrival. "Kace showed me the pictures of Jamison dressed as Santa for the children's hospital. I was contemplating whether he had needed any stuffing for that gut."

"Hey now." Jamison rubbed his stomach. "Don't insult the gas tank for the love machine."

A loud laugh burst from Kace, nearly drowning out everyone else's laughter. He exchanged glances with Jamison. They had debated whether they would announce their engagement yet. Christmas felt like a family thing they shouldn't overshadow. But with everyone together, they felt extremely close and real. It was like they read each other's mind. They shared a smile.

"By the way, guys. I asked Kace to marry me, and he shocked the shit out of me by saying yes."

"Oh, my God. Wow!" Joesph sounded genuinely happy for them.

"Congratulations, man." Shaw shook Jamison's hand.

"We'll be family." Joesph shoulder-bumped him.

"And to think, I set you two up. I should be a professional matchmaker. I honestly think I have a knack for it." Haven looked entirely too triumphant.

Jamison shook his head and put his arm around Haven. He squeezed her against his side. "You know, being a busybody isn't the same as having a knack."

She slapped his stomach.

He massaged the place where she had hit him. "Damn. I didn't say I'm not appreciative. If you hadn't shoved us together, Kace wouldn't have insulted me, and I wouldn't have realized I like being abused."

Kace couldn't stop laughing. He was so in love with this goofball.

Haven gave his stomach a pat. "So when is the wedding? Do you need help with planning?"

Kace's mind screeched to a bit of a halt. He hadn't actually thought that far ahead.

Thankfully, Jamison was good at handling things unexpectedly dropped on his head. "We have so much going on with the holidays, making plans to see everyone and whatnot. We haven't had time to sit down and look at dates."

Haven didn't dim. She clapped. "I'm so happy. Let's open the champagne I bought for New Year's. I can buy more later."

"Oh. We don't want to hijack your Christmas."

Haven waved away Kace's words. "This is family time. No matter what we're here for, we are together. We can celebrate more than one thing."

Jamison met his stare. The happiness and love in his eyes had Kace captivated. They were getting married. He couldn't believe his luck.

By the time they made it home to Kace's place, Jamison was exhausted. They had started the day with Kace's family. To his shame, that always made him a little tired. Kace came from money and his family was a pretentious bunch. It was obvious they never would have chosen Jamison. All he could do was smile and pour on the charm. He wasn't sure it was working. Their trip to Haven's—while better—was also draining. Maybe Jamison just wasn't that family-oriented. He didn't know. His dad hadn't put much stock in family—never taking him to any family gatherings. The only time he saw Joesph and Haven growing up was when Haven picked him up for weekend visits. So, Jamison never knew what was expected of him. He just showed up when invited. But Kace had been at his side every minute and that made everything better. Still, he was glad to be home.

"I can't wait to take a hot shower, put on my pjs, and do nothing all day tomorrow."

That sounded like heaven to Jamison. "Amen. In fact, I think that should be our Christmas day tradition."

They toed off their shoes and unpacked the gifts they had gotten. Jamison pulled out a funny coffee mug from someone in Kace's family. For a moment, they simply stared at each other. It was always like they shared one brain.

Kace broke first. "You should just leave it here, don't you think?"

While they hadn't talked about it, it seemed obvious he would live with Kace. Kace owned his house while Jamison rented. Not to mention, Kace lived in a gorgeous house in an upscale neighborhood. They just hadn't discussed any details since their engagement.

Jamison nodded. "That makes the most sense. All my things will be here, eventually."

They didn't look away from each other.

Kace didn't stop holding his stare. "Maybe all your things should be here sooner rather than later."

Jamison wasn't afraid of moving too fast. He was scared as hell of the hope Kace brought to his life. There was no one like Kace. No one would want him through sickness and his mental health the way Kace did. If he took his love and acceptance away, it might kill Jamison.

"Maybe so. I mean, I'm always here anyhow."

Kace nodded. "We're getting married."

The happiness in Kace's voice and expression made Jamison bold. "Hopefully, soon."

A smile exploded across Kace's face. "I'd like that."

The excitement made him impatient. "How about next—"

A banging on the front door followed swiftly by a nonstop doorbell ring had them turning toward the door. They exchanged a confused glance.

Jamison set the mug aside and waved for Kace to take a step back. The banging didn't stop. He checked the peephole. Horror raced through him.

"Who is it?" Kace's stage whisper cut through his shock.

"It's Lucas—"

Before Jamison could finish his sentence, Kace stormed toward the door and ripped it open like he planned to tear off Lucas' head. He, too, froze in horror. "What—"

Kace was shoved aside as two men helped Lucas inside. Blood covered nearly every inch of his clothing. Ajax and Hektor—two royal guards Jamison had hoped never to see again—dumped Lucas on the floor.

Ajax motioned toward him. "Fix him."

Kace looked horrified. "What the fuck? He needs a hospital."

"No hospital." He pulled out a gun and pointed it at Jamison. His steely gaze never wavered from Kace. "You fix Lucas, or I kill your man."

Kace took turns looking at everyone. He looked pale. Kace dropped to his knees at Lucas' side. "Yeah. All right. What happened to you?"

"Don't ask questions. Just work!" The barked words didn't cow Kace the way Ajax obviously hoped. He leveled a furious stare at Ajax. "I can't fucking fix things if I don't ask questions. So why don't you try shutting the fuck up and let me do my job?"

Ajax gave him a sharp nod.

Kace went back to Lucas. "I have to open this shirt. Tell me what I'm dealing with. Hold on." He looked Jamison's way. "I need my medical bag, plenty of towels, and lots of hot water."

Ajax shook his gun, obviously trying to remind Kace he was still in charge. "This one stays."

Kace could have frozen water into ice with the look he turned toward Ajax. "He knows where everything is, so he can get it the quickest. I'm starting to think you want your friend to die."

Jamison didn't wait for Ajax's permission. He jogged toward the hallway to grab Kace's things. Ajax wouldn't defy Kace. Kace wasn't weak. He would let Lucas die if Ajax hurt anyone. Jamison gathered as much as he could carry and dumped it at Kace's side before jetting into the kitchen to fill bowls with scalding hot water. He had no clue if Kace actually needed any of this or if he just bought time. Maybe he freed Jamison to call the police. He couldn't do that. Lucas ran drugs for the biggest crime lord in Atlantic City. His boss had everyone in his pockets. Considering that boss was a prince of The Republic of Serveno, he was untouchable. They were on their own.

When he made it back to the living room with two big pots of hot water and several washcloths, Lucas' shirt had been cut away and Kace wore surgical gloves. As he bent to set the pans next to Kace, he got the full picture and froze. It looked as if Lucas had been stabbed multiple times in his torso. Jamison fought the PTSD that tried to overtake him.

A pained through-his-teeth chuckle left Lucas. "Look out. Jamison is about to fall apart and steal the spotlight."

His sarcasm pulled Jamison back to reality. "Wow. Even when I could help save your life, you've decided being an asshole is more important."

"You used to like my asshole."

Kace froze for half a second. He didn't look at anyone. Then he went back to work. Unfortunately, he saw exactly how stiff Kace had become. Goddamn it. Lucas really knew how to wreck his life. Always had.

If Jamison stayed, he would let Lucas goad him until Jamison finished him off. It was best he left. He stood and turned away.

"His third best skill after cuddling and fucking—running away."

Rage had Jamison seeing red, but he still headed toward the kitchen. He heard Kace quietly speaking, but he couldn't make out the words. His pulse beat too loudly. He grabbed the coffeepot and filled it with water. This would likely take some time, and this was something he could do for Kace. He turned to find Ajax leaned against the kitchen island, looking relaxed and like he wasn't covered in blood.

"You know Lucas has always been a right cunt. That's part of what makes him irresistible. Don't let him get under your skin."

Jamison filled the coffeemaker and found the coffee beans. "Do you think I'm any happier to see you or to have you threatening to kill me... again?"

Ajax rolled his eyes. They were a gorgeous gray that nearly matched the slight streaks of silver through his dark hair. He looked as polished—even covered in blood—as the prince he served. "Please. Spare me, mate. I know you're not that weak. Since when does a gun at your head bother you?"

Jamison fought the urge to explode. "Since I left this life. I told all of you to stay the fuck away from me. This is a peaceful home. We have a nice, quiet, and normal life."

"To be fair, we're not here for you. It's hardly our fault you chose a man who is a doctor and knows Lucas."

He had been so upset, he had forgotten Kace knew Lucas. That got under his skin. "How does Lucas know Kace?"

Ajax smirked. "How does anyone know Lucas? Either drugs or sex. I doubt your boring little doctor has ever done drugs in his life."

Jamison looked away. His eye twitched. Things had been going so amazingly. He thought he worked on building a beautiful life.

"You always were a dramatic one. The gay scene isn't that big, if we're being real. Don't be stodgy."

Jamison growled. "I don't give a shit about what Kace did before me. Hell, he was one right choice away from marrying my cousin at one point. He's the best thing that's ever happened to me and we're likely as good as over, thanks to you people."

"Like I said, we're here for Kace's expertise. If you think you can keep him quiet about this, so we don't have to kill him, then there's no need for him to know about your past with us."

"What past?"

Jamison dropped his head to the counter and banged it softly when Kace's question hit. He really must have been a terrible person in another life. Jamison was constantly punished for crimes he didn't commit.

"He's stitched. I knocked him out. He needs blood, but I can't help you there. I've done all I can do under these conditions. If he lives through the next week or so, then he might live, but I think it's unlikely, given the circumstances."

"Is it safe to move him?"

Jamison listened to the entire conversation with his head down. He should go ahead and leave now. Kace would put him out soon.

"I wouldn't unless it's to a hospital—where he belongs. There's one guest room upstairs that has a bed. If you can get him up there and find a way to get blood for him, I'll do what I can until whatever happens happens." His voice hardened. "But if you ever pull a gun in my house again, *you* won't leave here."

Goddamn. Jamison straightened. He knew Kace was a badass, but fuck.

Ajax looked amused, but impressed. "I can get whatever you need. It should go without saying this is something you must keep to yourself."

"I'm a doctor. Whatever happens between my patient and me is confidential."

Ajax dipped his chin. "Give Hektor a list. He'll get whatever supplies you need. I'll stay with Lucas and play nursemaid until it's safe to move him." Ajax sounded confident Lucas would live.

Kace nodded. His gaze moved Jamison's way and back again. "That's fine. Clean up your mess." He walked away.

Ajax's laughing gaze moved Jamison's way. "He's a much better choice for you. You need a strong hand."

A thought hit. One that might go farther at saving Kace than any other—the same detail that had saved him. "He's Joesph's oldest friend."

Ajax gave him a sharp nod. "That explains a lot." He paused. A thoughtful look passed over his features. "Isn't he your cousin?"

Damn. Jamison forgot he had admitted Kace had dated his cousin and he only had one of those. "Yeah."

Ajax's eyebrows rose, but he didn't say anything else. They both knew Joesph was not only the prince's attorney but also his close friend. Prince Noir wouldn't allow any harm to come to that relationship—like killing Joesph's friend and soon-to-be cousin by marriage. They weren't completely helpless in this situation. At least there was that.

CHAPTER NINE

KACE WAS BEYOND FURIOUS. He didn't even know where to begin with trying to figure out why. He had been trying and working so hard on this relationship—always meeting Jamison more than halfway. Now, did he even know the guy? People had burst into his home, forced him to perform bare minimum surgery on someone he knew, and all while under the threat of watching them kill Jamison. What would happen if Lucas didn't survive? Kace honestly didn't think he would. They didn't understand how little Kace had actually done for the guy, simply because of the circumstances. He couldn't see the full extent of the damage without proper equipment and staff. Kace barely had enough supplies in his house to stitch what he could see. Soon, Kace would have a dead man in his house and if he wasn't arrested, he would definitely lose his medical license. For what?

He stormed from the shower and angrily dried his skin. Enraged didn't begin to cover his mood. He wanted to hurt someone. These people had ruined his life.

"I'm sorry."

Kace jumped at the sound of Jamison's voice. He hadn't realized Jamison was there, sitting in the dark. Kace was still too angry to let getting startled affect him. "Do you plan to tell me exactly what you're sorry for, or am I about to lose my medical license for reasons I'll never know?" Even he heard the fury in his voice. Kace wouldn't reel it in. He was done.

"You don't have to worry about that. Hektor and Ajax are part of Prince Noir Antonsen's royal guard."

He knew of the prince. Obviously, they had never met, because the guy was a prince, but Joesph and Shaw's law firm represented the guy. He had found that out only because the prince had been at Joesph's wedding and Haven was a gossip. "And?" They were over if Jamison stopped there. His temper and patience were gone.

"Lucas also works for Noir."

"None of this explains why they're here, threatening people, instead of getting proper help. That doesn't explain your part."

"I used to mess around with Lucas."

Kace shrugged. "Who hasn't, apparently."

Jamison visibly swallowed. "Is that why you two were together that night at the hospital?"

Kace rolled his eyes so hard, he nearly hurt himself. A man was about to die under this roof and Jamison worried over Kace eating in a hospital cafeteria with Lucas. "No. I told you, he was there for his sister. We ran into each other while buying food."

"Lucas doesn't have a sister."

Kace's shoulders fell. He swiped a hand across his eyes. It seemed he didn't know anyone.

"Back when I was with Lucas, he dragged me into his bullshit."

"What bullshit? You're being way too vague for my temper right now."

"Running drugs."

With nothing but a towel wrapped around his hips, Kace sat. Thankfully, the bed was there to catch him. "You ran drugs?"

Jamison shook his head. "He broke into my phone one night while I slept and stole all the contact information for my clients. Codes to their homes, gated communities, and alarms. He used that information to get to people who owed him money. Well, Prince Noir money."

"So the Prince is like a..."

"Crime lord, basically," Jamison supplied. "He runs all of Atlantic City."

Horrified was an understatement. "Does Joseph know this?"

"Of course. He can't protect him from what he doesn't know."

Fuck. He really didn't know anyone in his life. If tonight hadn't come, none of this would've ever been exposed. He would have lived his life connected to a crime lord without even knowing it.

"Anyhow, I might've never known he had done it if I didn't end up basically summoned to see the prince. He said he had dropped some hints to possible clients amongst the elite, telling them they should hire me. If they did, then he expected to be given all the same information on each one that Lucas had already given him on everyone else. In exchange, he would make sure no one ever suspected me, and he would stay quiet about how they were getting to these people in the middle of the night."

"Holy shit. How did you untangle yourself from that mess?"

Jamison shrugged. "I didn't, really. A few things just kind of went my way. First, I obviously told Lucas we were done. Then they eventually found someone with easier access to clients' information. It's also just risky to get that information from only one source. It wouldn't take long for people to realize I was the common denominator in their home invasions."

"This is completely insane. I'm surprised they didn't kill you. Maybe that's dramatic, but that's how it happens in the movies. You know too much, so you have to go."

"Joesph is apparently really good friends with Noir and not many people can say that. It would upset him if Noir killed me. Plus, he already has half the police force and all the judges in his pocket. What could I do? Who would listen to me? I'm just some crazy, PTSD-ridden veteran they could easily discredit." Jamison held his stare. "You being Joesph's oldest friend is really valuable right now. Don't forget that, okay?"

He read between the lines. He shouldn't deny their friendship. Joseph was the only thing keeping him alive.

"I'm sorry, Kace. So fucking sorry."

The fight went out of Kace. "It's not your fault. You heard what Ajax said. They were here for me. If I had never met Lucas, they wouldn't know me to terrorize me."

"It feels like my fault. Since you met me, it's been one thing after the other. I can't imagine how close you are to calling it quits. You've given everything. It feels like I've done nothing but bring you grief."

Kace's shoulders fell. He stared at the floor for a second. Kace needed a moment with his thoughts. Now that he was calm, he recognized a few things. In part, he was jealous. It was ridiculous, but this was the first time he had been confronted with Jamison having another relationship before him. He felt like an idiot for that. Then there was the idea of anyone threatening Jamison's life. His home had been invaded. He would likely lose a patient. There was just too much. He was overwhelmed. At the end of the day, he loved Jamison. This truly wasn't his fault. They had both simply found themselves in the wrong circle. He couldn't let Jamison think for a single second he would choose any existence that didn't include him. Kace took a breath and met Jamison's stare.

"The night you showed up at the hospital and I was with Lucas, I had just told him I had no interest in dating him. You literally showed up as soon as I said I wanted something real. I wanted a grown man who wanted to settle down and build a life. Then there you were, offering me exactly that. There couldn't have been a bigger sign that you're who I've been waiting for my whole life. If this is really forever, then it won't always be easy, but it will be real." Kace's voice shook with power at the vow. "You gave me that."

"I wanted to give you—"

The door opened, cutting off whatever Jamison had been about to say. "Blood is here."

Kace nodded. He fucking hated this. The blood was useless. Lucas would be dead soon. "Just let me throw on some clothes."

With a nod, Ajax left them alone.

Jamison stood. "Tell me what you need me to do. I'll help."

Kace grabbed the first clothes he found. "I guess just be on standby. Honestly, I don't know what'll happen from here." Once he was dressed, they headed for the guest bedroom. Lucas was still out. They had somehow found an IV pole to go along with the blood. Kace quickly worked to ready the bag while Ajax hovered.

The moment Kace stuck Lucas, his eyes opened. He blinked. "Where am I?" His voice was a raspy whisper.

Ajax chuckled. "You're at a reunion of your fuck buddies."

Lucas chuckled. It sounded like it hurt. "Jealous?"

Ajax smiled like the pair were truly friends. "Nah. All I have to do is walk into any room and ask how it is and someone could tell me. I don't need to experience the ride."

"Bastard." He blinked some more, as if he couldn't see very well. "Why do I feel so weird?"

"We drugged you. It's not like the good doctor has a hospital pharmacy in his house. We had to work with the hard drugs we have."

"You know I don't do that shit."

Ajax looked unbothered. "You are tonight. The shock has worn off. Without something, the pain would likely kill you."

Lucas licked his lips. "I'm already dead. That bastard is really going to let me die. After everything, he's fucked me."

Kace and Jamison exchanged a glance. He really sounded bad. The fear was setting in. He knew he was dead.

"Mom and I were supposed to celebrate Christmas tonight. She's probably scared out of her mind, wondering why I didn't come home."

Jamison looked furious. "Don't worry, I'll call her."

"Thanks. Don't tell her I'm dead yet. You know her heart is bad."

Jamison visibly swallowed and walked away like he couldn't do this for another second.

Kace started the line and watched the blood flow for a second. "Give that a minute and I'll be back." He quickly followed on Jamison's heels. Kace found him halfway down the hall with his phone to his ear.

"You listen to me. I don't appreciate having a half dead kid dumped on my living room floor, putting Kace's medical license at risk." It was obvious he had missed the first part of the conversation. He had no clue who was on the phone. "Don't interrupt me. I don't give a fuck what your boss has to do, but right now, he's letting this kid die. If he doesn't do something, he will fucking die. I don't care what it takes, but this isn't happening while I watch. If I call his mom and pretend like he's missing Christmas because he's tied up in a meeting or some other bullshit, and then these fuckers dump his dead body in a ditch, they will wish they never met me. I promise they'll never see me coming. You know I have the training to back up my threat. Fuck my mental health. I'll see all these fuckers dead."

Kace had never been prouder of anyone. No matter their history, at the end of the day, Lucas was twenty-eight. He was a real person, just as caught in the web of a powerful man as the rest of them were. Kace genuinely liked Lucas. He couldn't watch this happen, but he also couldn't stop it. His throat swelled as he listened to Jamison hang up one call and immediately make another to Lucas' mom. He sounded so kind and calm. It was obvious he had been more entrenched in Lucas' life than he let on. Kace had never felt more useless, and he had definitely lost patients before. This was different. Lucas stood a chance in a real medical facility. This was home-ec sewing class. This was just a slow death. He had internal injuries Kace couldn't fix like this.

The second Jamison disconnected his call, his phone rang again. He quickly answered. "Hello?" His gaze shot to Kace's. He nodded as if whoever was on the other line could see him. "Understood. We'll be ready."

Jamison stuffed his phone in his back pocket. "Come on." He steered Kace back into the bedroom like a man on a mission. He started barking orders as soon as he cleared the doorway. "Get ready. There's a helicopter on the way to transport Lucas to a private facility. We need to have him prepared to go straight out the door. Shaw is joining you to make sure no questions are asked."

Hektor jumped to his feet. "I'll wait outside and lead the way."

Kace nearly cried at the reprieve.

Ajax looked relieved as hell. He held Lucas' hand in a tight grip, as if lending him strength. "You hang in there, mate. Just a little longer and this'll be a bad dream."

"It's been a nightmare for a long time."

Kace looked away. He hoped he woke up soon and this night never existed. Help couldn't arrive soon enough. He had never felt so close to breaking down. Kace needed Jamison to hold him.

Lucas had never liked feeling out of control. He didn't understand how anyone stood getting high. He was out of his head and he hated it. Nothing would come into focus beyond Ajax's face. He felt the rattle in his chest. Death was so close, he could feel the icy grip. He supposed, as far as final sights went, Ajax wasn't a bad choice. The guy was one hot daddy. He had to focus on any wild thoughts he could. The movement of being transferred to a gurney and rushed down the stairs was absolute hell. He would cry, but fuck that noise. Lucas wasn't weak. He wouldn't be weak.

Everything went by in a blur until Ajax's face hovered over him again. Lucas tried to chuckle. He needed to be the unserious one all the way to the end.

"I've always thought you have great hair. Like a lion's mane."

A smile exploded across Ajax's face. "Jealous?"

"Nah. I'm just surprised you still have so much at your age."

Ajax roared with laughter, but his grip on Lucas' hand never lessened. At least he wasn't alone. He had always expected to go out in the worst way, totally devoid of comfort. But Ajax was here, so it was okay.

"Thank you." His eyes closed without his permission. He felt like he floated away, leaving his body behind. His voice sounded far away. "Tell my mom I love her and I'm sorry I wasn't better."

In a vague way, he heard people shouting, but it was distant, as if he walked away, leaving the scene behind. He had somewhere else to go. Maybe he would finally be happy.

As much as Jamison wanted to go to bed and put this bullshit night behind him, he couldn't stop pacing. He had a bad feeling if he closed his eyes, he would end up back in a war zone. Blood covered way too many places. They couldn't go to bed like this.

A crew showed up to scrub away the evidence while Kace silently moved in their wake, as if needing to do something. He had never seen Kace look so defeated. Jamison had never been more enraged. That was saying a lot.

His phone rang. Jamison checked the face. An unknown number appeared. It was too late for it to be anyone he didn't know. He answered, praying he wasn't about to have to call Lucas' mom again. The news would likely kill her.

"Hello?"

"You'll be happy to know Lucas pulled through surgery."

Noir's accented high-society voice wasn't the one he expected to hear. He didn't give Jamison time to respond. "If you think I'm an evil bastard who would leave most anyone to die, you're right. But in this case, I wasn't informed of how dire the situation was. You can rest assured that will be addressed. Did you actually threaten my life?"

Despite everything, Jamison smiled. He was so fucking relieved he would get to tell Kace Lucas was okay. Nothing else really mattered. "I might've been at the end of my rope."

"Mhmm. Well, it seems you hit that point at the right time. They lost him on the flight. Ajax did CPR until they had him on the table. If not for that, I don't think I'd take your threat so kindly."

"He's just a kid. I know you don't care who you exploit, but I do. He has a mom to care for and he's all she has. I realize none of that matters to you. It matters to me."

A loud, put-upon sigh rang through the line. "You really shouldn't presume to know what I care about. This is also the only time I'll pretend you didn't cross me. Tell your doctor Joesph will be by tomorrow with payment for his services. Next time, just call Joesph right away. No one knows me for a reason. I don't mingle at the bottom."

Jamison rubbed his forehead. Next time? Fuck. Kace was on Noir's radar now. There was no going back. "He's my cousin, so, you know. I have him on speed dial."

When Noir spoke again, Jamison heard the smile in his voice. "So defeated already. Don't worry. This isn't common for my people. I assure you; the problem has been handled." The barely suppressed laughter in Noir's voice sent chills down Jamison's spine. He had heard rumors Noir was a psychopath who made serial killers look merciful. It was likely a good thing cooler heads had prevailed by the end.

"That's good to hear. I'll let Joesph keep me updated on Lucas."

"Fair enough." The phone disconnected.

Jamison held it away and stared at the device for a moment. It had been such a crazy and horrible night. A Christmas Eve to remember, really. Fuck. He just wanted a normal life for once.

Kace wrapped his arms around Jamison from behind and kissed him between his shoulder blades. "Everyone is gone. I've locked up for the night."

"Lucas made it through surgery."

He felt the tension drain from Kace as he pressed his face against Jamison's back. "Thank God."

Jamison decided to leave out the whole dying on the way. Kace had already suffered enough. He turned and wrapped his arms around Kace. With his lips pressed against Kace's forehead, he breathed in the man's scent. "I've been thinking. How about Valentine's Day?"

"What about it?"

"For our wedding."

Kace cuddled closer. "That's not much time to plan, but I'm sure we could pull it off."

Jamison closed his eyes. He felt like crying. Jamison didn't know if it was relief or everything catching up to him, but tears pressed against the backs of his eyes. "You're the greatest thing that's ever happened to me. I hope you wake up every day knowing that. You're incredible."

He felt Kace take a deep breath. "Can we go to bed? I want to hold you."

"Yes. Please? I've never been more done with a day." He kissed the top of his head and then took his hand. Together, they turned out all the lights before climbing into bed. The moment he had Kace snuggled against him, every bad moment of the day vanished. "I just realized something."

"What's that?"

"My worst day with you has still been better than my best day without you."

A moment passed before Kace responded. "Valentine's Day sounds amazing. It would be really cute to have heart balloons and red roses—almost like a Valentine's party."

Jamison smiled into the dark. He was definitely a man in love. "I promise I won't cop out. Every year, you'll still get a Valentine's gift and an anniversary gift."

He felt Kace smile against his chest. "Same."

Jamison held Kace tighter. They had a plan. It felt great.

CHAPTER TEN

EACH BREATH JAMISON TOOK felt like it wasn't deep enough. He saw everything through a tunnel while Kace clung to the shower wall. His hips seemed to roll of their own volition. Nothing existed except the pull on his cock and the love in his heart. He was a mess.

Kace made sounds like he was in heaven. Jamison wondered if this was hell. He couldn't get enough. Surely lust should be sated at some point. Every day, he wanted Kace more than the last. At this point, he was a sickness.

"I'm too old to still want to fuck this often." He sucked air when he nearly came. Jamison had to wait. Kace had to blow first. "Why can't I get enough of this beautiful asshole? You drive me nuts."

Kace whined like he was close, but couldn't reach the edge.

Jamison couldn't take it. He wouldn't make it much longer. Jamison reached around and grabbed Kace's erection. He stroked. "You have to shoot that delicious wad, Kace. You've got me too fucked up. I'm ready to pound this ass and pump you full of cum. It's right there. You're too fucking amazing. The way you take this dick, damn. You have no idea what that does to me. I can fuck you any way I like, and you'll still moan my name." Pressure climbed his shaft. Jamison locked his back teeth and growled. He wouldn't make it.

Kace's asshole suddenly tried to violently suck him deeper. His cum painted the shower wall while Jamison's lungs seized. The sounds he made weren't sexy. He sounded like a dying moose. Jamison didn't give a fuck. His soul left his body. The pleasure rocking his cock had his stomach quivering. He couldn't stop slamming himself inside Kace, trying to pull out every drop of cum. Jamison wanted to watch him drip with it. Goddamn. He hadn't known a person could be this fucked up over another human being. Jamison would crawl across broken glass and nails to be with Kace. Everything about him was so far under

Jamison's skin, he thought he might lose his mind sometimes. No one had ever warned him about this kind of love. He hadn't known it existed, and it was so healthy. So fucking healthy. It was crazy to him just how calm, peaceful, and beautiful life was with Kace—when things out of their control weren't messing with them. All he had known was turmoil in relationships before him. Every day, he woke up thankful... and horny. Goddamn. He couldn't get enough.

His dick slipped from Kace's ass along with his cum. Jamison watched it happen. His stomach growled. He should be half dead. Instead, he already plotted a time and a way to have Kace again. He was hooked.

"Oh God. I can't move." Kace laughed as he made the confession. "I think my knees are locked in this position."

Jamison chuckled against Kace's shoulder as he kissed a path to Kace's ear. "It's a good thing you look sexy as fuck in this position, then. You'll make a good addition to the bathroom."

Kace shook with silent laughter. "Fuck. I love you."

"Mhmm. I love you too." He licked the shell of Kace's ear. "You're so sexy. It's irresistible."

"I can't believe it. It's like you didn't just fuck me senseless."

Jamison hauled Kace back against chest, ensuring Kace felt the way he was still hard for him. "I've told you a thousand times—I can't get enough of you. You're seriously like crack to me. I'm fucking addicted." He slid his hand down Kace's body and squeezed his cock.

"You're killing me here. We have plans today. You're making me want to blow off a perfectly nice lady. Is this who we've become?"

Jamison laughed at the dramatics in Kace's tone. "Yes. This is what you've turned me into. I'm a slave to your body. What sort of spell did you put on me? I'm a mess."

He loved the way it felt in his chest when he listened to Kace's laughter. Jamison couldn't stop smiling. He hadn't known love like this existed. If he had, every day, he would've been hunting desperately to find Kace. He couldn't live without this again.

"Tell me you love me, and I swear I'll get us out of here on time."

"I love you." Jamison heard the truth in his voice.

"Again."

Kace stroked the arm that still held his cock. "I love you."

This time, Jamison spun Kace and captured Kace's mouth so he could taste the words on his tongue. Maybe one day, he would get enough. But that day wasn't today, and Jamison seriously doubted getting his fill would ever happen.

The way Kace always smiled these days probably made him look like a crazy person. He was so goddamn happy, though. Life with Jamison was amazing. Even the hard days with him were worth every second.

He watched Jamison help Lucas' mom, Wendy, to the car. She was a sweet lady. While she could take care of herself, she was too weak to keep up the house or work. She could also drive herself to places, but she couldn't walk around enough to navigate once she got to where she was going. Without Lucas, she needed help. Lucas paid someone to clean their house and deliver food and whatnot. But he couldn't disappear and expect her not to notice or worry. She had to be told something, so collectively, they lied. As far as Wendy knew, her son had been hit by a car while crossing the street. Thankfully, Ajax had gone to her in person and dropped the news. He had ensured she didn't panic and damage her health. Jamison had volunteered to take her to see Lucas—after discussing it with Kace, of course. Kace thought he was the greatest man alive. He loved his caring nature.

At the car, Wendy smiled at the sight of him as Jamison helped her into the backseat of Kace's Benz. "Hi. You must be Kace."

They had spoken on the phone. She looked nothing like he envisioned. He didn't know why, but he had expected a frail-looking elderly woman. Maybe her weak health fooled his brain. She looked maybe ten years older than Kace's forty-two. Life really didn't care about age. Sometimes it just kicked you in the teeth.

"I am. You must be Wendy. It's nice to meet you in person."

A huge smile lit her face. She was beautiful. Almost ethereal. Lucas had definitely gotten his red hair from her, but her eyes were light green. "You too. I always loved Jamison. It's good to see he found a wonderful man. As much as I would've loved to have him as a son-in-law, my son is a bit of a free spirit." Her eyes flashed with humor as she made the claim.

A bark of laughter burst from Kace. She had no idea. "He's young. There's nothing wrong with that."

Jamison climbed behind the wheel after stashing Wendy's walker in the trunk. "All right. Is everyone ready?"

"As I'll ever be," Wendy responded from the back seat. She sounded exactly like she tried to stay upbeat in the face of something awful. "I still can't believe this happened. Have you seen him? Does he look terrible? That Ajax man was pretty vague about the situation."

The doctor in Kace kicked in. "He'll be okay. Craig Lock Memorial is the best private-care hospital around. He's in great hands there."

"I notice you didn't answer my questions. It's worse than Ajax let on, huh? I thought that man looked like a salesman. He's probably worried I'll sue this prince he works for."

Kace bit back a laugh at the fire in her voice. No matter her health, she was obviously a fighter. "I haven't seen him since he was hospitalized."

"Oh." She sounded exactly like a light bulb lit in her head. "Ajax said Lucas was treated by a doctor on the scene who saved his life. That was you."

Kace hated lies. They compounded and bit people in the ass. "Yeah. That was me." Damn. He was relieved as hell when they reached the hospital. The last thing Kace needed was an elaborate story he couldn't keep up with.

Wendy was quiet on the way up to Lucas' room. He practically felt the worry rolling off her in waves. There was no mistaking which room belonged to Lucas. A guard, wearing all blue with a royal seal on the shoulder of his jacket, stood outside the door. He barely spared them a glance before stepping aside.

Jamison lightly knocked and poked his head inside. "Hey, I've got your mom."

Kace knew Jamison's announcement was a warning, giving Lucas time to cover any sign of his actual injuries. He stepped inside immediately. Kace understood why as soon as they cleared the door. They had Lucas covered in heavy, heated blankets from chin to foot. Nothing could've told Kace more. Lucas had lost nearly all his blood. Even after infusions, he would have trouble regulating his body temperature for several reasons. There was no hiding how dire his situation actually was. Several machines had wires running beneath the covers along with a catheter and IV lines. He looked exactly like the trauma patient he was.

Wendy gasped at the sight of him. "Oh, my God."

"Hey, Mom." Lucas sounded awful.

As Wendy pushed her walker across the room, Ajax vacated the seat next to bed, offering it to her. She flashed him a smile before focusing on Lucas again. "Hey, baby. I knew you sounded weak on the phone, but I didn't expect all this. You should've told me how bad things really are. What are the doctors saying?"

Lucas blinked like he was still out of his head. Likely, he was drugged to the heavens. Kace, being Kace, checked the IV bags. Yep. He had the good stuff.

Lucas' hand slipped from beneath the covers. "It's okay." It sounded like it cost him everything to speak, much less stay awake.

She kissed his hand before squeezing it and hanging on tight. Wendy focused on Ajax. "Tell me what they're saying. Don't sugarcoat it."

A kind smile touched Ajax's lips. He was the general of the royal guard. That role took more than physical training. He was polished—expected not to embarrass royalty. "He'll make a full recovery, but it'll be a long one. Glass and metal sliced through his upper torso in several places, damaging internal organs. He lost a lot of blood. It'll likely take months for him to be back on his feet."

Wendy looked pale.

Kace couldn't stop looking between every person in the room. Months was a long time to keep up this lie. It was obvious they understood that and gave the best story they could to explain his wounds.

"This sounds expensive. Not that I'm worried about the money as much as my son. I just know him. He'll try to do too much too soon to keep us above water. Lucas never thinks about himself."

Kace immediately focused on Lucas to check his reaction to his mother's claim. He had already passed out again.

Ajax kept his heavily accented voice soothing. "Don't worry about a thing. His Royal Highness will take care of every-thing. Lucas was working for him when he was hit. Prince Noir intends to ensure he rests, heals, and doesn't stress while he recovers. Everything will be fine."

"Mom." Lucas was awake again, but barely.

She stroked his arm. "I'm right here, angel. What do you need?"

"I'm sorry I ruined Christmas."

Kace looked Jamison's way.

A muscle ticked in Jamison's jaw. It was obvious he felt the same way Kace did. Lucas shouldn't be in this mess.

"I love you, baby. This isn't your fault. Just get better. We'll still do Christmas at a later date. You didn't ruin anything."

"Love you too."

He was gone again before the words died on his lips.

Wendy swiped her cheeks. "You boys don't have to stay. I'll stay."

Everyone cast glances at each other.

Ajax spoke up first. "Lucas wouldn't want you endangering your health for him."

"I'm a grown woman. Don't worry about me." She lifted the lid on the seat of her walker, showing the compartment underneath. "I have extra clothes and my meds." She motioned toward a bag that hung from her walker. "I brought snacks. It's worse for my health to go home and worry nonstop. At least here I can rest with my son."

She had a point. They couldn't very well toss her from the building, especially without making Lucas worse. Kace wouldn't say it, but the doctor in him knew. There was still a good chance Lucas could die. They had him in ICU for a reason. Modern medicine was an amazing thing, but they had kept him from getting immediate care and there was no telling what damage that had done.

Someone had to be the one to let Wendy be the mom. "Jamison and I will head out. There're too many people here. If you need us, just call. We'll take you back home or grab whatever you need."

Wendy swiped her cheeks again. "Thank you. I don't guess anyone would've bothered to bring me if you hadn't. It's my job to take care of him."

Kace got it. "I know. Call if you need anything."

Ajax jumped in. "I've been assigned to stay with him. So I'll be here if you need a break or food."

Wendy flashed him a kind smile. "Thank you. I appreciate it."

With her settling in for the long haul, Kace and Jamison said their goodbyes. They made their way back to the car in total silence. The heaviness of the situation weighed on them. It had been two days since Lucas had been dumped in their living room. Somehow, it felt like a lifetime. They equally felt helpless in the face of so much.

Jamison broke first. "I know Lucas can be a real asshole, but this is bullshit."

Kace got it. Despite everything Lucas had done to Jamison, what choice had Lucas had, really? He was no more able to say no about stealing those contacts than Jamison had been about continuing to hand over information. Some things were just too big. Plus, he had his mom to consider. How many jobs were there where he made enough money to care for her while also being present? No matter how shitty the situation was, Kace got it. He didn't judge him.

"It sounds like they plan to take care of him. At least there's that."

Jamison nodded. He stared straight ahead but didn't start the car.

"Do you want to go back inside and hang around? I understand if that's what you need."

Jamison looked his way. "No. He has his mom. That's what he needs. I just hate that this happened, and I really don't understand why I'm this upset about it. He's my ex. I don't love him. It was never that serious. This is just... *ugh*."

Kace got it. "He's young, and this is un-fair. I get it. Plus, it extra feels like it's on our heads because he was brought to us. But I think he'll recover, and he'll make sure we remember exactly why you couldn't stand him. I can't imagine any-thing keeping him down for long."

Jamison smiled. "Actually, I have a feeling he'll give Ajax hell. Ajax seemed more than a little involved."

Kace laughed. "Well, Lucas has made his way through the gay scene."

Jamison laughed before letting out a loud, long sigh. "Jesus. I'm tired of drama. Can we get married and be normal again and have back a quiet life already? Seriously, I'm just ready for that life with you."

"Okay."

Jamison's gaze sharpened. "I need clarification on your response."

Kace shrugged. "Okay. If you want to get married. Let's do it. It'll take us a couple of hours to drive to Delaware and get a marriage license. We'd only have to wait overnight to get married there. We'd have to wait three days if we got one here."

Jamison blinked. "You're serious."

"Of course. If you genuinely don't want to wait, then okay. Let's do it."

A huge grin split Jamison's face. He leaned across the console and stole a deep kiss before starting the car. He threw it in reverse and met Kace's stare. "Okay."

Kace settled deeper into his seat and took a breath. They were on their way to happiness forever. Why would he argue with that?

Keep an eye out for the next Atlantic City's Most Wanted, *General.*

About the Author

CHARITY PARKERSON IS AN award-winning and multi-published author with several companies. Born with no filter from her brain to her mouth, she decided to take this odd quirk and insert it in her characters. One of her greatest loves is writing morally gray characters. You'll find them scattered throughout her hundreds of titles.

*Nine-time Readers' Favorite Award Winner

*2015 Passionate Plume Award Finalist

*2013 Reviewers' Choice Award Winner

*2012 ARRA Finalist for Favorite Paranormal Romance

*Five-time winner of The Mistress of the Darkpath

Connect with her online:

*Sign up for her newsletter: https://bit.ly/charityparkersonnewsletter

*Join her readers' group on Facebook: http://bit.ly/CharitysTribe

*Website: https://www.charityparkerson.com

*A list of her social media accounts and giveaways all in one place: http://hy.page/charityparkerson

www.ingramcontent.com/pod-product-compliance
Lightning Source LLC
Chambersburg PA
CBHW070926250626
47159CB00009B/3141